Joy to the Junction!

5 Small Town Christmas Stories that Inspire

J. A. Bouma

Introduction

It's the most wonderful time of the year in Mill Creek Junction. The Christmas season roars into the small fictional Midwest town like it does into most of our lives, but in ways unexpected.

A year ago, I'd been kicking around the idea of creating a fictional smallish town in West Michigan for several months, thinking it could be a fun way to tell the stories of people living life while exploring faith, taking a page out of Stephen King's playbook with Castle Rock, Maine, and John Grisham's Clanton, Mississippi.

Then the Great Pandemic of 2020 hit, and it seemed like the perfect time to kick off the project! After all, I was stuck inside like most people with lots of time on my hands. Figured I should keep busy, because as they say: idle hands are the devil's tools! Sounded like great fun anyway, spending my newfound time with a new set of characters in a new world outside my normal world that had been blown up by a crazy virus, but also something different from the usual story world of my existing fiction.

Thus was born Mill Creek Junction, as well as a host of

characters who show up in the Christmas-themed collection of original short stories set in the small Midwest town.

Christmas ranks right up there as my most favorite time of the year. Living in the Midwest myself, I have fond memories trudging through knee-high snow on the way to the bus stop. Of course, much of my pastime was filled with building snow forts and getting into snowball fights with the neighbors (I'd say neighborhood kiddos, but often the adults were the victims of my assaults, too!). That isn't even touching on the hours I spent perfecting my mad sledding skills breaking the speed of sound on a mile-high schoolyard hill.

Then there are the Christmas traditions. First on the list was cutting down our tree from a Christmas tree farm the day after Thanksgiving—a tradition I've carried through to my own family. Christmas Day was magical, when my sister and I would wake up at 6 o'clock on the dot to get everything ready for the morning festivities: turning on the Christmas tree lights, striking up the fireplace to full roar, getting the cinnamon rolls baking. Then at 7 a.m. sharp, we'd wake my parents singing a Christmas carol, dragging them out of bed with those cinnamon rolls (and filling mugs of coffee for my bleary-eyed parents) before ripping open our presents. And, like throwing up our fresh-cut Christmas tree the day after Thanksgiving, I still carry on that tradition for my kids, dragging my kind-hearted, understanding wife along with me—still enticing with cinnamon rolls and, for her, a cup of tea.

Oh yes, for me, the Christmas season is the most wonderful time of the year!

I know that's not the case for everyone. For many, for a variety of reasons (often connected to family), the Christmas season can be hard, brutal, painful even. Which is why I wanted to put together a collection of heartwarming stories of people living life and exploring faith in this fictional town to offer a bit of inspiration for the season. I hope it also recaptures some of the magic of Christmas, with its sights and sounds, it festivities and traditions.

First story is Max Blade's story, owner of the local watering hole, Max's Place. He's a real believer in Santa Claus, or at least the magic and good vibes he and his legend invoke during the season. But there's another legend from one of his friends that competes with the Jolly Ol' Soul that doesn't sit right. And that's when things get...interesting for Max—and the Junction!

The second story is straight from my parental heart. As parents, we all want to give our kiddo the world, especially at Christmas. Some are barely able to offer them a single Hot Wheel or American Doll, let alone a tree-full of presents. Sometimes the circumstances align just right that another gift is required. What they call a life lesson. Which is a far better Christmas gift than a Hot Wheel or American Doll anyhow. If you're a parent, you'll understand the drama of the story—which an incident from my own childhood inspired!

Story three stars one of my favorite characters, Johnny Pope. He's a former priest turned private investigator who stumbles into a caper at his favorite diner. An old flame and her granddaughter need his help, and he reluctantly offers it. What he discovers in the end reminds him, and us, of what the season is really about: forgiveness, even for the rottenest of souls.

The fourth story is a bit of a departure. For Gideon O'Donnell, love is in the air this Christmas season—and an engagement right around the corner. Except he stumbles into a mystery and a crime a few days before Christmas.

Look for a happily ever after that more than makes up for the frightful circumstances. But also for the reminder of how much the season isn't all roses and rainbows. Sometimes dark shadows creep into the happiest season of all.

Then the finale, which is fitting: Pastor Peter Daniel Young is responsible for the town Christmas pageant, and he has in mind a retelling of the original Christmas story, the one about Jesus' birth. Except it's not coming together quite right. After all the trouble he goes through, all his work, he's reminded of a simple, oft-forgotten lesson, one he himself needed to hear and relearn. The one at the heart of the 'reason for the season,' as they say.

So here's to the most wonderful time of the year. May these stories give you a chuckle as much as a dose of inspiration for the Christmas season. May they warm the heart as much as entertain the mind. And may the Christ of Christmas find you this season, wherever you are at.

Joy to the Junction, joy to the world.

Joy to you and yours!

Grace and peace,
~J.A. Bouma • November 2021

Story 1

Santa Claus v Old Man Bayka

"Twas the night before Christmas, when all through the bar. Not a creature was stirring, not even a—"

I stopped at the edge of the stairs leading up to the stage camped out at the east end of the room still hopping with conversation and laughter greased by beer and burgers and a good dose of Christmas cheer.

Think, Max Blade, think! What rhymes with bar?

I glanced around my place, Max's Place, the bar that'd been in my family since before the Great Depression and near well since the founding of Mill Creek Junction. Smelled like it too, now that I think of it. That old, woody smell of earth and spice and tar. With those peanut shells ground into the hardwood something fierce, and all that spilled wheaty pilsner beer and even stinker moonshine Gramps made during Prohibition still flaring up its barley and rye. Add to that the lingering stench of a century worth of cigarettes and cigars and cigarillos from our friends south of the border working the Junction celery fields sticking to the walls like a bad habit—pun intended!—it's no wonder peeps still came back night after night.

But back they came. Especially this night, Christmas Eve.

The lights all strung up around the joint probably helped draw 'em flocking like the salmon of Capistrano—the reds and oranges, greens and blues all mixin' together to set the holiday mood just right. Not those new-fangled LEDs fancied by suburban folks, mind you. The big fat bulbs Granny and Gramps had strung up around their shrubs, the ones Millennials fancy in that ironic sort of throwback way.

Mine were strung up around the ceiling, zig-zagging this way and that, another pile of 'em thrown around an itty-bitty Christmas tree rivaling good ol' Charlie Brown's. Found her on the side of the road just at the edge of the Junction off Main Street heading back with a midnight snack from Meyer's General—Ben & Jerry's Phish Food; because sometimes a man's got to sit down with a tub of the best dang ice cream in the middle of December and a good Lifetime Christmas flick, wearing sherpa-lined slippers and a complementary bathrobe. And there she was, just growin' up along Route 55 like it was nobody's business. So I plucked her up off the ground and threw her in the back of the Golden Nugget, then zoomed back and set her up on stage where Marvin and the Gang play most weekdays before heading up for the Lifetime flick.

Anyway, back to glancing.

"Bar, bar, bar..." I muttered below the din of late-evening bar chatter. Then I gasped, one end of my mouth curling upward.

There it was. Back at the—bar, of all places.

Jar!

I considered it a hot second.

Not a creature was stirring, not even a jar?

Then tossed it to the curb.

Move on Max…

I glanced up on stage, missing Marvin and the Gang and regretting giving them the night off, a rolling playlist of Christmas crooners keeping the patrons happy—when a smile spread across my face.

Guitar!

Not a creature was stirring, not even a guitar?

Would have to do on such short notice.

I smiled and continued on my jaunt circling the joint, making sure my patrons were having a jolly good time this snowless Christmas Eve. Which got my dander up yet again after complaining to the Big Man Above about not a cotton pickin' centimeter of the white stuff this time of year. How do you celebrate Christmas without snow, for goodness' sake!

Now that's downright blasphemous! Although, I guess my peeps in Vegas don't quite care about that sort of thing. And I'm pretty sure the Christ child himself had a zero-snow birthday, given he was born in Israel, or Judea, or Palestine, or wherever the politically correct term is nowadays. That's not even touching on the fact no way was baby Jesus born during December!

Irregardless—or regardless, I always mess that up—I kept up my saunter across the hardwood floor my grandpa had first laid and coated with enough shellac to give you a high for the next century, the boards throwing up a creek, then another, along with a reminder to check them things out come the new year, figuring globally warming or climate change or whatever cray-cray governmental policy was responsible for Michigan having a no-snow Christmas and irritated to high heaven about it.

But first things first...

My jaunt through my place, Max's Place, on Christmas Eve, muttering to myself my tale like a crazy person, as I did each year.

"The stockings were hung by the chimney with care—" literally, as was the case on the mantle of a genuine fireplace up on stage. "In hopes that Saint Nick soon would be there."

Someone slapped me on the back as I passed a rambunctious bunch.

I turned to find Chief Roller jawing it up with Mayor Goodall and a few fellas from the city council. Always fellas, they are. Wished Claudia Pentwell would have won instead. Now that would have been a sight to see, Mill Creek Junction's first female mayor! Oo-wee, yes, sir, Gramps woulda turned over in his grave, for sure! But the good mayor somehow eked out another win, continuing the family legacy stretching back to Mill Creek's founding.

"Howdy, Chief," I said, nodding and grabbing the man's hand. I offered a round of howdies to the fellas around the table and continued on. After all, I had a poem to write.

"The patrons were nestled all snug at their tables," I said, continuing on around the room, "a beer in one hand and a burger in the other, commanding Max Place's staples."

I twisted up my face as I reached the bar at the back, my poetic chops not carrying the same ring and gravitas as the original. But it would have to do.

"Burt and Sheila in their aprons and I in my suit—"

"What you mumblin' 'bout, Max?" Burt asked, carrying two plates. He set them down before two patrons. They turned around. Gideon O'Donnell and Annabelle Kirkland. The Junction's resident attorney and local prosecuting attorney, just paling around on Christmas Eve like we don't know they're an item. Of course.

I said, "Oh, nothin', Burt. Just waxing poetry."

"Mmm-hmm. Is that what ya doin'…"

"Nice suit, darlin'!" Sheila said, walking up behind. She was wearing a pretty little thing herself, a black skirt and white blouse with a bit of ruffleage under her serving apron. Legs on a fifty-year-old gal never looked so good!

I whistled and gestured at her from head to toe. "Nice outfit, yourself! You just get in?"

"Been here an hour or so, getting the regulars situated for the big night before the big day, you know how it is."

"Sure thing, Sheila. Night of Christmas Eve in these parts is bigger than the typical Thanksgiving Eve. Wonder why that is?"

She laughed. "Because them religious Midwest folk know they can't get drunk on Jesus' birthday!"

I chuckled. "Probably right on that."

"Haven't seen you around yet this evening. Where you been?"

"Waxing poetry," Burt said, surely as ever, spitting *poetry* out like a bad peanut.

I turned toward the man and tossed him a frown. "Yes, Burt. *Poetry.* Us Renaissance men aren't ashamed to wax it now and again. Besides, it's a little tradition I have every year. I walk the joint and quote *'Twas the Night Before Christmas,'* adding my own little spin to the thing."

Burt leaned against the bar's edge, throwing a towel over his shoulder. "You better watch yourself, chief. You're liable to get your backside sued by the brothas estate if you ain't careful!"

I scoffed. "Fat chance. It's been in the public domain for years."

"Mmm-hmm. If you say so, chief."

I tossed my hand against Gideon's shoulder, the resident lawyer of the group. "Tell 'em, Gideon, I'm in the clear, right?"

Gideon took a breath and blew it out of pursed lips, then leaned back on his stool with a look that made my gut go watery. "I don't know, Max. You might be in hot water if you're not careful. These sorts of estates, with well-known intellectual property, can be pretty litigious."

"Really?" I said, eyes wide and wishing I had a beer to wash down my dry throat.

He laughed, throwing back his own beer. "No, you're fine."

I sighed and smacked his arm again. "And here I was fixin' to comp your next round."

"What's that about, anyway?" Sheila said. "Saw you wandering around muttering to yourself. Figured you ate a bad bean burrito earlier in the day."

That got the group going.

"Ha, ha," I said. "Very funny. I'll have you know the tradition stretches back to my pops, who used to wander the place singing Christmas carols on Christmas Eve. Sorta tradition."

"Thank God Max took up waxing poetry instead," Gideon muttered into his beer glass before throwing the rest back.

I took the empty glass in one hand and smacked him on the head with the other. "You're done for the night for that one."

"Hey, I was just getting started!"

"As far as traditions go, that's a weird one, Max," Burt said. "Even for you."

"Is not!" I protested, filling Gideon's glass only halfway, then plopped it down in front. "That's for the wisecrack."

Sheila patted my arm and chuckled. "It's not weird in the Max Blade sort of way."

Gideon and Annabelle cheered that one, raising their glasses and throwing back a swig.

"Don't let them get you down, Max," someone said on the other side of Annabelle. Looked like Peter Young.

"Oh, hey, pastorman. Didn't see you there."

He raised his glass. "You go waxing as much poetry as you want. Especially on Christmas Eve and in your own bar."

"Damn straight! And what about you all, then, if you think my tradition's weird? I'm sure there are some doozies sittin' around here."

Mariah Carey started belting "O Holy Night" while my peeps went silent.

"Well, we get chocolate letters," Sheila said, breaking the ice.

"Chocolate letters?" I asked, raising a brow and one end of my top lip.

She smacked my shoulder. "Don't look at me that way? Yeah, chocolate letters! Us Dutch folk give one another the first letter of our first name in white, milk, or dark chocolate."

"So instead of sending letters to Santa," Annabelle said, "kids get literal letters from the jolly man?"

"From Sinterklaas, but yeah, that's right."

I smirked. "If you ain't Dutch, you ain't much, I guess."

"Damn right!"

"That's not so much weird as it is tasty," I said. Gideon

drained his beer and handed it to Burt. I took it instead and went to fill her up. "What about you, *O'Donnell*? With a name like that, you've gotta have some weird Irish traditions in that home of yours."

I handed him his drink. He said, "Thanks, but you're forgetting I'm adopted, and my adoptive parents are descendants of black slaves."

I reddened a shade, embarrassed I'd forgotten that tidbit of his story. "True, but their...well, slave owner was Irish, right?"

"That's right. But that don't make me Irish."

"So what' your background, then?" Peter asked.

Gideon took another swig and shrugged. "Don't know. Mama—err, my birth mom left me at the Junction fire station forty years ago."

"So, for the sake of argument and Christmas fun," I said, pouring myself half a glass, "let's say you're Irish. Any weird holiday traditions up that family tree?"

He laughed. "Not unless you consider stocking up on booze the day before Christmas an Irish tradition."

We all laughed at that one.

"One thing I remember my dad doing as a child was dressing up as Santa."

"That's not weird!" I protested, throwing back a swig of beer.

"Well, when you think about a rail-thin black man wearing a flannel robe and cotton balls stuck to his face with vaseline, that's pretty dang weird!"

Almost lost my beer on that one. "Yeah, that's pretty funny."

"And also pretty historically accurate," Peter said next to Annabelle.

"How so, pastorman?" I asked.

"Well, the original Santa Claus we think of was Saint Nicholas."

"Sounds about right," Annabelle said.

"Except he wasn't some white European."

"He wasn't?" I asked, bewildered, my childhood flashing before my eyes.

"He wasn't African, either, but he was Turkish. Or at least the bishop of Myra of modern-day Turkey. So his skin would have been a more burnished bronze hue."

"How do you like that…"

"Pretty cool, actually," Gideon said.

Peter laughed. "He also punched a heretic, so that's doubly cool."

"No kidding?" I asked, amazed that my childhood hero wasn't who I thought he was.

Pastorman nodded and threw back a swig.

"Now that's weird!"

"I'll drink to that," Peter said, raising his glass.

"Alright, you want weird," Burt said, leaning against the bar. "I'll give you weird."

I said, "Hit us with your weirdest Christmas tradition, Burt."

"You heard of Krampus, the hit movie with the same title?"

"Yeah, that flick was bangin'!" The others groaned and threw peanuts at me. "What? It was!"

Burt twisted up his face. "What's the matter with you, boy? The movie was about some European holiday devil."

"Wait a minute," Annabelle said. "Isn't that the one who wears animal skins and horns and roams the streets to punish kids who've been less than nice?"

Burt nodded. "Mmm-hmm. That's the one."

She leaned over the bar top and smacked my arm. "What a creepster, Max!"

I jumped back in time to avoid her hand, then raised my glass with a smile. "Missed me."

Burt chuckled. "Well, believe me, Krampus ain't got nothin' on what I grew up with."

"And what's that?" Gideon asked.

"Well, let's just say my earliest Christmases weren't all sugar plumbs dancin' in my head, but a high dose of fright."

"Fright?" Peter said.

"That's right. Fright. On par with Max's favorite horror flicks. What were they? Saws 1 through 15?"

The others laughed—at my expense.

I frowned. "Ha, ha. Very funny, Burt. But just remember who cuts your paycheck, dude."

"Touché, chief."

"But what's this about fright? During Christmas?" Peter asked.

The man nodded. "Mmm-hmm. During Christmas."

I threw back a swig of beer. "How? I mean, Santa. Baby Jesus!"

"Naw, it wasn't Santa Claus that gave me the fright. And not the reindeer or elves, since I never got any dose of those parts of the Christmas tradition. No, what gave me the heebie-jeebies was because of my ancestors."

"Ancestors?" Annabelle said.

"That's right. My parents are first generation Africans."

"What were they again?" I asked. "Libyan, Latvian, Lithuanian—"

"Liberian, knucklehead!" Burt moaned.

"Same difference..."

"Hey, I think my adoptive parents have Liberian ancestry," Gideon said. "Brought on slave ships over from West Africa."

"Wouldn't surprise me none," Burt said.

Gideon scooted to the edge of his seat now with interest.

"What scared the living daylights out of me," he went on, "was the Christmas tradition of the so-called dancing devils that pranced around the streets during Christmas."

I put up a hand. "Hold up, hold up, hold up! What the heck you talkin' about? Dancing devils during Christmas?"

"That's right," Burt said. "They come out to dance, and in return they demand gifts. Now, these weren't the European white man devils, but the bush devils of my parent's homeland."

"That's crazy talk!"

"And pretty weird," Gideon said.

"You're telling me!" Burt said. "Gave me nightmares for years, so that I hated Christmas. That is, until Mama and Papa explained the devil isn't considered evil. It's more a force of power that can be used to right society. Bring justice to the community and right injustice."

"Like *the* Force?" I asked.

He chuckled that deep, husky belly laugh of his. "Something like that, chief. But the thing about it is, it's like a Santa reversal Claus."

"A whatchamacallit?"

"A reversal Claus. Instead of bringing gifts for the little tykes, the devilish visitors would come seeking a gift from the family. My family would go to some of these events with drumming and commotion as these boy actors darted toward people in the crowd trying to get something, anything. Eventually they'd move on, going door to door to collect their bounty. Usually cold beers and cash for the dancing devils."

"You saw all this as a kid?" Annabelle said.

"Sure did. Fascinated and frightened me, it did."

"But it's not Christmas!" I protested.

"It's a Christmas mash-up is what it is, plumbin' the depths of African spiritualist tradition while combining it with global Western traditions, like plastic Christmas trees and Santa Claus, too."

"Sounds cool to me," Gideon said. "The Junction could use a Christmas mash-up like you're talking."

I threw him a frown but held my tongue. I was as multi-cultural as the next guy, drinking my far share of Red Stripe and fair trade Rwandan coffee, but—come on! Devils on Christmas?

"Hold on, Burt," Sheila said. "You say Santa makes an appearance?"

Burt nodded. "Mmm-hmm, sure does. At the town Christmas show, the real star is Old Man Beggar."

"Old Man Beggar," I said, twisting up my face.

"The two Dudes of Christmas would go at it in a toe-to-toe competition to see who could put on a better performance. Old Man Beggar's got this big belly," Burt said, leaning back and putting his hands over his own generous gut. "Dresses up in raggedy clothes."

"That's Santa Claus!" I interrupted.

"No, sir, Max. Santa's pimped out in fancy new threads."

I crossed my arms in a huff, muttering, "Sounds like Santa to me."

Gideon drained his bear and passed it off to me for another. "I don't care what Max says, Burt. This Old Man Beggar sounds cool. Especially the face off with Santa.

Hey, maybe we could get a match up on Main Street this year!"

Annabelle laughed. "Wouldn't that be something! You could be Santa, Max. And Burt, you could be that Old Man Beggar guy."

"Like some old Western duel, right on Main Street!" Sheila laughed.

"That'd be for real funny!" Burt said. "But really it's about begging for gifts more than it is about showing off."

"What do you mean by that?" Peter asked, draining his own drink and asking for another.

Burt leaned against the bar top again. "Well, another name for Old Man Beggar is Old Man Bayka. Country devil, he is, walking up and down the streets and even going door-to-door on Christmas day."

"Begging?"

"Mmm-hmm. For gifts, money. Scares the youngsters something fierce."

"I'd bet."

"But adults greet him with food and drink. 'My Christmas on you!' he cries out."

"Say that again?" I said, pouring a full drink for myself now, a nice ale stout. I was gonna need it.

"Instead of saying 'Merry Christmas!'" Burt explained, "Old Man Bayka calls out 'My Christmas on you!' or 'My Christmas is in your blood!'"

"What's that mean?"

"Basically, he's saying, Give me something nice for Christmas! It's mostly a friendly greeting, but it's more about shedding light on issues of injustice. A heartfelt plea for food and water. Wealthy Liberians don't much care for it, and usually they're the ones that are hit up to sort of point the finger at the stingy Scrooges who refuse a request for help. So Old Man Bayka's performance becomes a commentary on the stinginess of the wealthy."

Gideon smirked. "Mill Creek Junction definitely could use a dose of such consumeristic confrontation."

"You're telling me! I have half a mind to bring Old Man Beggar to the Junction myself!"

Annabelle leaned over Gideon with a grin and said to him, "You and your windmills, Don Quixote."

Gideon threw her a frown, "I'd say tilting toward the windmill of injustice is pretty worth it, Miss Assistant Prosecuting Attorney!"

And she threw it right back. "Confronting people about their consumerism on Christmas is a bit much."

"Whatever it takes…"

Peter blew out a breath and threw a Jackson on the bar top. "Sorry, guys and gals, but that's enough for me."

"I should probably get back to it myself," Sheila said. "Chief Roller's gonna throw the book at me if I don't refill his Miller Lite."

Burt snorted a laugh. "Man deserves to have the book thrown at him for his choice of beer."

We all shared a laugh at that one. Then Gideon and Annabelle handed me their cards to cash out.

"Should probably get back to the farm myself," I said, closing out their tabs.

"First things first, boss," Burt said, grinning from ear to ear with open arms. "My Christmas on you, Max!"

I laughed, but returned the gesture. "Merry Christmas, Burt!"

He sauntered back to the kitchen, then the two Love Birds left.

I got back to making my Christmas Eve rounds around the joint trying to find a word that rhymes with burger, eager to complete my Blade tradition before the big on the docket for tomorrow.

"Merry Christmas!" I shouted from the Golden Nugget, taking a swig of brew and shouting even louder a second time: "Merry Christmas!"

My aging, sagging Plymouth Breeze gave a grumbling protest as I goosed the engine forward. Hit a pothole the other day, then hit something on the way out, jacking up my undercarriage. Sounded like a crotchety old garbage disposal, the noise was so loud.

No matter. The jingle-jangle of bells I'd mounted up top masked most of it as I pulled at a rope dangling through my window.

"Merry Christmas!" I bellowed again between sips of more brew. I was gonna need it for what came next.

I was moseying down through Springdale Road jutting west off from Main Street, a nice tree-lined street with turn-of-the-century craftsman homes and colonial throwbacks to the Junction's founding. Normally leafy green during the summer, the boughs were heavy with a snow after a right Nor'easter dumped on us something fierce last night. Apparently, the Big Guy Upstairs heard my complaints!

Pulling the Golden Nugget to the curb, brakes squawking up a backup chorus to my grumbly, mumbly muffler, I parked the Breeze and got to work, throwing oping my door and fishing out a large red sack passed down through the Blade generations.

Last time this thing was used I think it was the Christmas after 9/11, then before than the height of Nam and clear back through the Second World War and Great

Depression. The Blades had a tradition of passing out goodies to the good folks of Mill Creek Junction during hard times. Simple staples like toothbrushes and cans of coffee, cookies and candy.

I figured this corona-crazy year was as hard a time as any to go passing out goodies to my neighbors, my friends.

So off I went, nose freezing and feet hella-cold in the stiff leather black boots passed down to me by Gramps. Thankfully, the rest of me was right toasty, seen as how I'd stuffed pillows at my belly and back underneath my cherry-red Santa suit smelling of Pops's cigars and Gramps moth-balls. Hoped the duct tape held!

Crunching across the freshly fallen snow, a big fat grin spread between my rosy cheeks and breath riding high with a head of steam, I started up Springdale Road. I adjusted the grip on my sack of goodies, because boy was it heavy! Full of chocolate bars and balls and candy, even some tooth-brushes and toothpaste thrown in.

When what to my wondering eyes did appear, but a hobo sans eight tiny reindeer! Tall and a belly rivaling my own, a black cowboy hat sitting awkwardly on his big head, a man was shouting "My Christmas on you!" in front of a white two-story Victorian house with black shutters and smoke rising from a stone chimney, one hand outstretched and the other shaking some sort of drum instrument—with a black sack thrown over his own back!

When no one came, he reached into the bag and set something down on the driveway, then sauntered back down and out into the street, presumably heading to bother another poor family knee-deep in wrapping paper and presents.

Did my peepers betray me? Looked like Old Man Bianca, or Bayka, or Beggar, or whoever-the-heck-it-was!

The gale!

I frowned, an irritation rising within. "There's only room for one fat Christmas man, pal," I growled to myself. "And you ain't it!"

So I hoisted my sack of toys over my shoulder and took off after the man, barely feeling my frozen feet now but not caring a lick. Santa's honor was on the line! No way was no devil gonna ruin Christmas. Not on my watch!

Time for Santa to whoop Old Man Bayka's keister back to Libya or Lithuania or wherever the heck he was from.

WWE smackdown style!

"Burt!" I shouted, my voice carrying down the tree-lined road, boughs sagging with the weight of the freshly fallen Christmas snow.

The man stopped cold, dead center of the street between houses, face masked with something straight out of that *Scream* movie that gave me the willies for half the '90s!

"Yeah, I'm talkin' to you, ya big lug! I know it's you, so let's give up, pack it up, and go home and leave peeps to their gleeful participation in America's Consumer Industrial Complex. That's the true meaning of Christmas, pal!"

Bayka slowly turned toward me while I was planted thirty yards away, the pair of us staring one another down, OK-Coral style, but without the fancy shooters.

He said something to me across the way, but the mask—well, masked it from my hearing.

I tilted my head. "What's that you say?"

"My Christmas to you!" Then he started toward me, that twisted face and tilted cowboy hat, an opened tattered gray coat and holey pants pulled high over his generous gut and held by red suspenders. At least he got that part right, but the rest was just shameful!

Regardless, Burt didn't sound right, voice higher than

normal. Probably toked back a bit too much eggnog before he went traipsing through the Junction Christmas morning.

So I went after him, throwing down my bag of toys and charging Burt, some sort of anti-Christmas spirit taking over me. But really it was a pro-Santa spirit reclaiming the honor of the tradition.

What happened next was unexpected. Reaching him with an outstretched, shaking finger, I slid on a patch of black ice and plowed into the man.

We went down in a heaping pile, Burt's hands slapping at me to get off. Which riled me up so that I started pushin' and shovin' at him to get off of me. My right hand caught his *Scream* mask just right, and I ripped the thing clear off!

What I found underneath shocked my socks off.

To my surprise, he was not the man I expected. Not in the slightest!

I sat up and twisted up my face in confusion. "Gideon?"

The man looked madder than a wet hen, his face red and mouth bunched up. Then he started swatting at me again like a boxing kangaroo! Had to raise both arms to defend myself.

"Stop it, man! You're gonna bust my nose."

"Then get the heck off me!" Gideon shouted.

"Alright, alright!"

I rolled off him to the pavement cold and wet with melted snow, a shiver ratcheting through me now at the chill.

Gideon stood and shouted, "What the heck was that for?"

"Me?" I shouted back. "What the heck was that all about? The carrying on, the devil costume, nabbing presents from poor kiddos—dressing up like Old Man Bianca, for goodness' sake!"

"Old Man Bayka!" Gideon spat at me. "And I wasn't nabbing presents from poor kiddos. I was giving them out."

I furrowed my brow and jutted my head out with confusion. "You were?"

He showed me his sack, which looked nearly empty now of balls and small games and crayons. "When I didn't get anything, I have something instead."

I was aghast! How dare he!

"Bu—Bu—But that's my job!" I stammered. "This town's only big enough for one holly-jolly ho-ho-ho man, pal. And you ain't it!"

"Ha!" Gideon laughed. "You don't have the corner market on gift giving on Christmas, Max!"

"No, but Santa sure does! And besides. Nobody wants some weird tradition from Lithuania."

"Liberia!" Gideon shouted with wide eyes, that vein popping now. "Besides, Santa is only one weird tradition among all the others, knucklehead."

"Yeah, well, it's America's weird tradition, pal. And we do weird traditions like none other! Why do you care so much, anyway? It's not like you're Libyan."

"Liberian," he said again, sounding tired now, defeated even.

"Sorry. Liberian, then."

Taking a breath and huffing out a head of steam, Gideon motioned to the side of the road. I followed, and we plopped our keisters down in the snow, our warm bottoms quickly growing wet with melted snow.

"I guess I wanted a tradition to call my own," he said.

I shook my head, confused. "What do you mean? You're American! Which means you've got Santa and presents and mistletoe, for crying out loud!"

Now he shook his head. "No, I mean a *tradition*, from

my family, my ancestors. All your talk at Max's Place yesterday got me thinking about how I don't know anything about my own heritage, being adopted and all."

"But you've got your Mama and Pops."

"Who have their *own* heritage. Libyan, with a side of Irish slave owners thrown into the mix! Sheila has Dutch chocolate letters, and you," Gideon said, motioning my way, "you've got this Santa getup from the Blade clan stretching to the Junction's founding. But when Burt went on about his own people's heritage, this Bayka character, well…"

His voice faded, his head dropped with a sadness to him.

I said, "You thought you found some heritage, some tradition you could put on like a bad Christmas sweater?"

He chuckled. "Something like that. My parents never mentioned anything about Bayka, but I thought if that's the heritage of my adoptive family, the traditions of my parents' ancestors, then why not make them my own?"

I nodded, feeling bad now about getting all worked up and bent out of shape about it.

"So I thought I'd show up and walk from door to door, like Old Man Bayka would in Libya and spread his Christmas message with hands held out and—"

"—and shame people knee-deep in wrapping paper and presents into feeling bad about their merriment?"

He shrugged. "Shedding some light on the inequity Christmas can bring, which seemed to be what Old Man Bayka was up to."

I considered that, catching a glimpse of my sack filled with goodies I was planning to give away, the thin crimson fabric soaking wet now.

Sighing, I said, "I suppose we were spreading the same sort of Christmas cheer."

Gideon looked at me. "What do you mean?"

"Well, I was giving gifts to those in need, while you were asking from those who had. Seems like the meaning of Christmas to me, just said in different ways, from different ends of the spectrum. And I suppose our traditions reflect those different ways. Doesn't make one better or truer than the next. Just different."

He smiled. "I liked that."

I offered a grin back before grabbing his shoulder and giving it a squeeze. "Sorry for giving you a Christmas beat down."

He laughed. "If that's a beat down, then I'd hate to be on your side in a barroom brawl."

"Hey, I can hold my own. After all, I do own a bar."

"I suppose."

We sat on the side of the road, silent for a long time, our bottoms swimming on melted snow now.

Until the honking of a siren and whirling of the reds-and-blues startled us both.

"Merry Christmas, fellas. How's it hangin'?"

It was Chief Roller, rolling up on us in his cruiser, bringing it to a stop at our feet. He dipped his rotund eight-ball head of his on that pedestal of a neck and flashed us an annoying grin of pearly whites.

I smiled and threw up a nervous chuckle. "Uh, hey, chief. What's up?"

"Got a few calls from confused, if not nervous, neighbors. Said something about some Santa versus Satan street fight."

"Old Man Bayka," Gideon corrected, head down and sounding gloomy.

"Whatever. You two alright? Do I need to throw you in the drunk tank, on Christmas Day of all days?"

I shrugged. "Couldn't hurt none."

Gideon flashed me a frown. "No, chief. We're fine."

"You sure? I'm sure the Prosecuting Attorney's office would be more than happy to have a chat with you down—"

"I said we're fine." Gideon took a breath after biting the chief of police's head off, then held up a hand. "We're good, right, Max?"

I nodded right quick. "Yep. Good."

The chief eyed us, twisting that bald head of his this way and that, those sausage fingers resting on that steering wheel of his.

Then he threw his cruiser into gear and pulled away, shouting, "You both have a nice Christmas, you hear?"

And I promptly threw up the bird.

Gideon laughed, and we high-fived each other, two friends back together again.

He stood and held out his hand. "What do you say we get back to it?"

I eyed it skeptically, then threw him a furrowed brow. "Get back to what."

He held out his arms and waved them around the neighborhood. "Spreading Christmas cheer across Mill Creek Junction."

"Wait, you mean both traditions?" I asked, skeptical.

"Side by side," Gideon said with a smile.

"Sounds positively American, don't it?"

He chuckled. "Exactly."

"My Christmas to you, Max," he said.

I smiled. "And to all a good-day."

Then we got to it. Spreading Christmas cheer.

Santa and Bayka, arm in arm.

One tradition to another.

Story 2

The Better Gift

hat to get, what to get.

I turned down another aisle, that awful Muzak droning on in the background with a bunch of dead crooners dreaming of a white Christmas while us shoppers were just dreaming of completing our shopping list.

Or in my case, finding that perfect gift that would make Jamal sing.

I pushed through the aisle of balls and sticks and nets, assessing, discerning, sizing up but knowing this wasn't it. The boy wasn't much into sports. Not that he wasn't athletic. Got that from his daddy. More that the interest wasn't there. So I kept at it, pushing down another aisle while Chicago came on belting out "Feliz Navidad." Where was a good gospel choir when you needed one?

I huffed and kept pushing, humming my own tune as those boys and girls kept at it. I was on a mission for just the right gift. Knew it was a suicide mission, seen as how it was the week before Christmas. But one could hope. And with the world bleedin' Amazon dry, figured stopping in to

Meyer's General was a shoe-in for a good deal on at least something from Jamal's list.

I figured wrong. The place was picked over like a bad Southern BBQ dinner, it was so bad. Cornbread and collard greens, the bird and all just plumb picked over!

But roaming the aisles I was, tryna find something that would put me in my son's good graces and not mess up the poor boy's Christmas. But all that was left was balls and nets and Barbie dolls. And Lawd knew I wasn't getting any of them for my Jamal!

A voice from behind hollered, "Mrs. Morgan. Was there anything I can help you with?"

I spun around to find Freddy Meyer standing behind me, chocolate brown slacks with a blue shirt and matching chocolate suspenders.

"Goodness! It's Mr. Meyer himself."

He smiled, saying nothing.

"A regular Junction celebrity!"

Now he looked to the floor. "Oh, I don't know about that. Just trying to offer the Mill Creek folk honest-to-good-ness deals on what they need most."

I raised a brow and took a step back. Sounded like a mighty fine ad script for their next TV or WeShare social media jingle. I've seen the man popping up in my newsfeed here or there. Nearly makes me jump out of my drawers every time!

I cleared my throat and smiled. "Looking for a Christmas gift for Jamal, but not having much luck."

"Oh. Well, have you seen the TX-1000?"

"The T-who-what-now?" I said, twisting up my face at the foreign-sounding language.

He chuckled and smiled. "The TX-1000. A smart-phone-controlled drone."

"Uhh, no..."

"Well, it's all the rage, as the kids say nowadays. Your kid will be the talk of his Mill Creek Junction neighborhood."

"For real?"

"Oh, yes, really."

"You're not just turnin' up the Fred Meyer charm to make a sale."

He chuckled and pulled at his suspenders with his thumbs. "Mrs. Morgan, if you don't buy it someone else will. I just want to make a child smile on Christmas Day. Come on," he said, snapping his suspenders against his skin-and-bones chest and motioning with as skinny of an arm. "Let me show you."

He skipped down the aisle—yes, with a skip in his step! I was skeptical, but followed after. Couldn't do much else but follow after. Not with Jamal's Christmas on the line.

We reached an aisle that had been nearly cleared of any remaining signs of life. Looked like the toilet paper aisle the day after lockdown back in the spring, it was so bare!

Fred Meyer put his hands on his hips and searched high and low, his beady little eyes squinting and his face scrunching up something fierce.

Until he gasped and threw his hands up in the air right before he reached down low, getting on his knees and shoving aside some Barbie mobile and Lite-Brite.

Then he stood, grinning and presenting to me a green drone.

"Sometimes customers like to hide products," he said with a laugh. "They come back later, thinking it'll be there. Sometimes it is, sometimes it isn't. Anyway, I'd bet my bottom dollar that this is what would make ol' Jamal Morgan's Christmas sing!"

I took the drone and frowned, assessing the packaging, not really knowing what I was looking for, but knowing ol' Freddy Meyer was the expert in these sorts of things.

"Yes, ma'am," Meyer went on, "this here drone has been flying off the shelves. Well, not literally," he added with a chuckle, "but yes, indeed, it is the hottest toy this season."

I looked at him with a raised brow. "Then why is this one left?"

He shrugged. "Call it luck. Call it Providence."

"Something wrong with it?"

Now he frowned and craned over the drone. "Can't image there is. Of course, you've got until the end of January to return it if there is something amiss."

I frowned again, returning back to the radio controlled drone, or bluetooth drone, or whatever-the-heck-controlled-the-dang-flying-machine drone that was half my day's wage at Millie's on Main. Was hoping for a bonus this year, but not planning on it. Not with the 'rona virus that'd done the place a world of damage to the financial books.

But I held it, feeling the weight of the contraption. Seemed hefty enough. I turned it around, admiring the green paint job and decals. I flipped it over, not knowing why but only that if it felt right, it must be alright. Sort of like kickin' the tires on a new car you was interested in buying. The four blades looked pretty cool. And I could see Jamal flipping his head when he opened it on Christmas, which made my mama heart warm just thinking about it.

Then I flipped it back over and stared at it from the top, a slow smile starting to reflect across my face in the plastic from those awful white fluorescent bulbs shining down from above. Jamal would just love this contraption, I just knew it! And better yet, it would be a surprise; he wouldn't see it comin' by a long shot. Those make the best Christmas gifts, in my opinion. Can't stand it when people spell out in song and verse their exact Christmas wish list, hand it over, and expect you to just shell out the clams and hand over the goods, gift-wrapped and all. Might as well just write you a dang check, it's so ludicrous!

Nu-uh, no sir. Christmas ain't about getting what you want. It's about me buying what I want you to have!

I took a breath and nodded at myself before looking up at Fred Meyer himself.

"I'll take it."

Fred smiled wide, flashing those white teeth from those WeShare ads that got me every time. He took it from me and said, "I'll have it wrapped for you, all special like."

I thanked him, then he walked away.

Then I prayed to the Lawd Almighty I was doing the right thing.

"Stick 'em up!" I say to the Indian in my left hand, the green cowboy in my right doin' all the gunslinging.

I know it's not politically correct, calling them Indians, whatever that means. Mama says they're Native Americans, but the plastic package said Indian, so that's what I call him. Mama and Daddy picked it up when they went to Mackinac Island this past summer. She said she was hesitant, but didn't understand why. I thought it was a perfectly fine gift for a seven-year-old boy. So did Daddy. And since he's the keeper of the purse in our house, even though he has a wallet and Mama has the purse, I got the goods.

Mr. Cowboy was part of a posse, you see. Came roaming in from the countryside that was my living room looking to bag some Indians—apparently another politically incorrect thing I said, according Mama. But she wasn't here. She was out at Meyer's General doing what Mama's do best. And I was patrolling the countryside looking to bag some Indians. Hey, a kid's gotta do something to pass time, especially when the Parents refuse to get me a Nintendo Switch. Maybe this will be the year they spring for a digital device, as they call them.

Probably not.

So off I go, crawling on all fours for the cardboard fort that was keeping my citizens safe from the Indians, looking for backup for Mr. Cowboy while Mr. Indian shoots his way out of his bind and calls for backup. Not a real fort, mind you. Just an Amazon box I swiped from the garage that was headed for the garbage truck. Love me the Zon! And combined with Alexa, it's like our house is a regular *Willie Wonka and the Chocolate Factory*, fulfilling every wish at my command!

Now, Mama and Daddy aren't on the same page with that one. They've had a chat with me a time or twelve about ordering Legos and M&Ms and a new iPad that Daddy promptly returned. I told them they should put a passcode on it if they don't want me using it, but they didn't listen. Probably couldn't figure it out if their life depended on it!

In my Amazon-box fort, I round up the reinforcements when something catches my attention. I poke my head up above that cardboard at something I hear.

I know that sound. It's the garage door, I just know it.

The sound of Mama coming home from Meyer's General!

Bet if I sneak over to the side door real quiet like I can catch her by surprise and catch a glimpse of a Christmas present I just know she was fixin' to buy!

So I creep through our dining room, if you can call it

that, then on through the kitchen to the side door leading to the garage. I slip just inside a teeny-tiny bathroom standing next to it and wait.

I hear Mama's car door slam shut. I hear her grumbling a curse as she rummages around the car, going in and out of doors, collecting what sounds like bags. Then I hear her clomping up the wood steps to the door, fumbling with her keys, more cursing she says is potty-talk when I say the same.

Soon the door is opening, Mama is coming inside, back-side first with both arms weighed down by bags from Meyer's General.

Then I jump out and shout: "BOOOO!!"

"LAAWD JESUS HAVE MERCY!" she exclaims, jumping clear out of her skin, bags of groceries thumping to the floor as her feet literally leave the ground.

I double over laughing. I laugh and laugh until it hurts.

Then it does hurt.

Mama grabs me by the ears and drags me to my feet, slinging a string of words I didn't even know existed, but very clear my little prank wasn't appreciated.

"Ouch!!!" I scream.

"Yeah, you best be screaming, boy! Ida have half a mind to stuff a sock down that throat of yours soaked in gasoline and light it on fire!"

Yep, she's mad.

She lets go in a huff and crosses her arms, looking up at the ceiling to catch her breath while tapping an angry toe on the floor.

I sink my head to my chest. "Sorry, Mama."

"Sorry? That's the best you can do, boy? You near well gave me a heart attack!"

As she stands over me, my eyes wander down to the

ground, and over to one particular bag containing some-thing big and boxy. Definitely not Cheerios or any other kind of food.

Looks like something for Christmas!

Smiling with my tongue hanging out, I start for it. "Is that one of my Christmas gifts?"

But Mama intervenes, a massive arm flinging out with her baseball-mitt palm blocking my way.

"Don't even think about it, boy!" she says in her husky don't-even-think-about-it-boy voice, putting an exclamation point behind her threat.

"But, Mama..."

"Don'tchoo Mama me, Jamal! Ima goin' straight to my bedroom and hiding this where you can't snoop. And I swear, if you go peeking and you see your gift, Ima taking it back. Gotme?"

I go to answer, but Mama presses a finger to my mouth.

"Think about your answer very, very carefully, Mal. You gonna listen to your mama and O-B-E-Y me, baby?"

She holds her finger there, a bit too long and close for comfort. Then she pulls it away, my mouth still open, that squinty eye of hers fixing me like a death ray.

Then I say, "Yes, ma'am."

She raises a brow at me. "You promise?"

I nod quickly. "I promise."

She nods and walks away, turning down the hall to her bedroom.

We'll see about that.

Then off I go, planning to take a peek.

Minutes later, from my room, I hear Mama come out of her bedroom and close the door. Then she saunters back to the garage side door where I hear her hoist the Meyer's General bags on her arms and saunter back to the kitchen. Before long, she's hummin' a Christmas carol—"I'm Dreaming of a White Christmas," I think; never know with Mama—while she puts away the goods.

That's when I spring into action.

I know I only have ten, maybe fifteen minutes. So I've got no time to lose.

Tiptoeing to Mama's and Daddy's bedroom, I look behind me down the hallway, keeping an eye open for Mama and an ear to her crooning while testing the doorknob.

It turns.

I smile. Success!

I push through the door and shut it behind, then start making my way around the room.

Doesn't take long, because it's not much bigger than my own, but I start with all the usual spots: under the bed and behind the dresser before the obvious next target: the closet.

That's when I see it.

If I said the closet door was standing wide open, I'd be lying. It was cracked, but a slice of light coming from the window behind was angling through the opening just right that it hits four words that made my heart race.

RONE.

I don't know what no RONE is. But I do sure as the day is long—I learned that from Daddy—know what a DRONE is!

Heart thumping in my chest, I tip-toe over to the Parent's door and peer outside. Mama is humming only the good Lawd above knows what while she puts away the groceries. Daddy is nowhere to be found.

Coast is clear!

I turn back to the closet and pad over, coming in for the kill.

Now, truth be told, I know without a shadow of a doubt that she woulda shut that dang thing right up tight. No doubt in my mind.

Yet there it is: cracked open like a man with his zipper clear down to his toes!

So I tip-toe back to the closet and throw the door open *post haste*. RONE is still staring at me through a Meyer's General plastic bag, so I gently peel back the opening with a pen I found lying on the floor. That's standard procedure on NCIS. Avoids leaving fingerprints and all. So I figure that is the right move here.

Never know with Mama...

I get on my knees now, scrunching up my face for a better assessment of the situation when—

What should appear before my wandering hands and wondering eyes?

A TX-1000!

I'd seen that bad boy advertised on WeShare when Mama wasn't looking. Looked hotter than a hot plate in a slick green that was ti-*ight*! With not one, not two, not THREEEEE! But F-O-U-R turbo-venting whirling blades!

Holybamoly, Batman, I've struck gold! Or rather, Mama struck gold. I can't believe it. Mama actually did it. She pulled the trigger after dropping hints once a week, sometimes twice a week that this was *the* gift. The *creme de le creme* of gifts.

I plop down on my bottom now, a drunken smile playing across my face, though I didn't really know what that meant. Mama had said something to that effect once when Daddy surprised her with a new Dyson vacuum cleaner. Definitely no TX-1000! Mama's got nothin' on me!

Speaking of which...

It's awfully quiet out there now.

I jump to my feet and tip-tow back over to the Parent's bedroom door.

Mama starts belting the latest Shakira. In fact, she's belting my name down the hallway—clearly wondering where I'd gone.

Time to wrap this up. So Mama can wrap it up!

Mama's voice is louder now, coming toward her bedroom. I glance back at the closet door, wondering if I should close it. A split-second decision...

Nah. Mama won't notice it open compared to how I found it. Parents miss those kinds of details. That's why kids rule the roost in the end.

I crack open the door and slip out, taking a breath and slowing my pace—

—when I smack into Mama coming around the corner.

"Whatcha doing, boy, runnin' into me like that?"

"Sorry, Mama! Didn't see you."

"Didn't see me? Comin' from where?"

I see her look over me—I am only four feet tall—and into her room. Then I see her face turn an ugly shade of purple, her mouth falling and jaw clenching and steam dang-well coming out of her ears now!

She looks at me, square in the eyes with a gaze so powerful my eyes are thrown to the floor.

"Did you go into my room, Jamal?"

My eyes go big; my mouth goes bigger searching for a lie. But I can't tell it.

Don't need to say nothing anyway, because Mama knows. She always does.

Her face falls and turns an even frighteninger shade. Not the red or purple when she gets angry. A slightly lighter shade. Her shade of sadness.

Her lower lip starts to quiver and she swallows hard. Now my lower lip starts to quiver, and my eyes fill with the same sadness as Mama.

"Go to your room," she whispers, closing her eyes and standing still.

I don't move for the longest several seconds. It's not that I don't want to obey, it's that I can't. I'm frozen with the realization I made Mama cry. I hurt her.

She says it again: "Go to your room, Jamal."

I go to obey but stay and say instead, "Mama—"

"Go to your room, boy!" She shouts this time, with a rising rage.

Now I move, spinning and running to my room.

I want to take it back, take it all back. My disobedience, my peeking and seeing and ruining her surprise. It would mean more to me than a hundred drones if I could put things back to the way they were before.

Instead, all I can do is flop on my bed and cry.

Lawd, what am I gonna do?

I sat on my bed, throat constricted with emotion and lower lip quivering with the same. A box of Kleenex was half empty with my tears, the tissue scattered about on the floor. A clock *tick-tock*ed in the background, keeping time in the silence and driving me mad. Never did like that thing, but now that I was alone with my regret, I just wanted silence. Not the dadgum reminder that every tick that tocked brought me one step closer to what I knew I needed to do, but didn't want to.

I brought a tissue to my eyes again, then blew my nose, shaking my head and heaving a heavy sigh. I couldn't believe the boy had gone and done it. Gone and disobeyed my direct order.

What I couldn't believe more, though, was that I threatened to take his gift back if he peeked in the first place! Now I was tied to my promise. Why did I ever think to do such a thing? What kinda Mama takes back her kid's best gift—a drone of all things?

In the moment between tears, a still-small voice broke through: *'The kind of Mama who takes the long view with their child and loves them more than a drone, of all things.'*

It was the Spirit of the Lawd himself, I could feel it!

'Besides,' the Spirit went on, *'the life-lesson you'll teach Jamal will be worth more than the drone he'll outgrow in a few months.'*

Now that hit on it. Made me feel a bit better, too. But just a bit. Wouldn't make it any easier what I knew I needed to do—both with talking to Jamal and then hiking it back to Meyer's General. But it reminded me there was a purpose behind it: the boy he would become knowing that Mama's word meant something when I instructed him not to peek, and so should his word mean something when he promised he wouldn't peek. But more than that, there are consequences for our actions.

I just hoped he understood it was all out of love.

Lawd, let him know it's all out of love!

That dadgum clock ticking in the background filled the silence as I worked up the courage to do what came next. I heard Jamal thrashing around down the hall, so I knew I better get to it before the boy popped!

So I stood, taking in a deep breath and sighing a heavy sigh—of regret, of dread.

Sometimes being a parent sucked!

But I sucked it up and walked out of my bedroom, down the hallway, and stood before Jamal's room door.

I took another breath, gave a soft knock at his door, then opened it.

Prayin' to the good Lawd above that he gave me the confidence to finish what I started.

For Jamal's sake. And my own.

I'm standing at my window looking out onto our yard piled high with snow. It came later this year—something about global warming, but Mama and Daddy think that's a crock —but now it's like a blizzard.

There's a soft knock at my door before it opens. I spin around, heart jolting into my head and pounding a mean beat.

Mama shuffles inside, face drawn and still that lighter shade of sadness.

I don't move, so she comes to me.

She says, "I want to try this again, Jamal. I want to ask you what I asked you before and I want you to tell me the truth, alright?"

I quickly nod, hoping my cooperation will stay Mama's hand.

"Did you go into my room after I told you not to?"

Again: a quick nod.

"Did you open my closet door?"

I know what to say, but I don't say it.

I just stare at her.

"You saw it, didn't ya."

I take in a breath and look to the floor now, my eyes closing with the knowledge of what came next.

She took in a breath of her own, then sighed. More like a huff, really, before she gasped a sniffling breath through her nose.

I open my eyes and look up. She is biting her lip and holding a hand on her hip, the other one dabbing her eyes with a tissue.

Mama is crying.

I hate it when Mama cries. More than hating when Mama cries, though, I hate when I *make* Mama cry!

Don't know how or why, other than not being honest with her from the start, and taking a peek in her bedroom. But why all the drama? I don't get it.

"Baby, sit down," she says, finishing up with her eyes and taking a breath.

I edge to my bed then hop on top, my Spiderman sheets a mess I now regret. Remember Mama had said to make my bed that morning. I hadn't. Now I wish I had.

She gets to her knees and looks at me full in the face.

Which means something bad is coming. Something deep.

She takes another breath, then swallows and gets this look about her. Like she's made up her mind about something, and she is ready to go at it.

"Jamal, now when I came home, you remember me telling you not to go in my room, right?"

I nod quickly. Figure the cat is out of the bag and tryna stuff it back in makes not a difference.

She presses her lips together and nods back. "And you

remember me telling you that if you did go in my room not to look in the closet, right?"

Now I swallow before nodding back, saying nothing more.

Another lip press, another nod. "Ima gonna ask you something, Jamal, and I need you to be real honest with me, aight? Real honest."

She holds my eyes with hers and nods back, knowing what is coming and not sure if I can do what she is asking.

"Did you see something you weren't supposed to see in my closet, baby? A gift from Santa?"

Can't do it any longer. That's all it takes.

Can't stomach looking at Mama anymore, so I look down at Spiderman instead. But then all heck breaks loose.

It's my lip that goes first. Jumpin' and jivin' like Mama's iPhone is blaring away. Then it's my eyes, water streaming down my cheeks before chest starts searching for air. Then I'm bawling like I was four again.

She doesn't reach in for a hug, doesn't pat my knee, doesn't do any of the Mama stuff Ida expect during times like this.

Instead she says, "Now, Ima gonna have to do something that neither of us are gonna like." She stops, then she takes a breath. "Ima returning the drone you saw back to Meyer's General."

It's like someone flips the switch on the world, and the whole thing starts spinnin' in slow-mo. I see my childhood flashing before my eyes, and that kickin' bluetooth-controlled green drone with a camera and four hover blades that went as high into the sky as a 747 getting yanks from my fingers!

"*Nooooo!*" I scream, my face still wet and mouth feeling salty now from the taste of guilt. I'm fighting for my life, for my very childhood. Mama can't take back that drone. My neighborhood rep is on the line!

"Ima sorry, Jamal, but the decision's been made. As soon as we're through there Ima marching straight back to Meyer's General and returning the contraption."

"But—but—but—"

Mama puts a finger to my mouth like before, the corners of her eyes starting to drip now. She says, "Breaks my heart seeing you like this, Jamal, but I'm standing firm on this."

"But it's a drone!" I say through sobbing tears now. "It's the best gift I ever could have ever gotten. I don't want you to return it. I love it!"

"I know, baby. And I was so excited to give it to you," she says calmly. "I guarantee you, child, this hurts me more than it hurts out. I bought that gift out of the goodness of my heart, out of my love for you. I told you not to peek, because I wanted it to be a surprise. The best you ever could have ever gotten, as you said. But you disobeyed, and there are always consequences for disobedience. Not just with Mama and Daddy, but with life. And learning that life-lesson now is worth more than the drone."

I think that's crap, but I don't say nothing in return. Can't, I'm so sad and sobbing.

"Come here, baby..." Mama says. She draws me close, holding me and patting my head. "None of this is gonna change my mind, Jamal, the tears and sobs. Though I certainly understand it. My heart's breaking for me as much as you. Not that I don't love ya, and not that I don't sympathize, but it's for your own good."

I pull away and wipe my eyes, my brow scrunching as I search her face.

What I see tells me she's telling the truth.

And maybe she's right.

I sigh and wipe my eyes some more. "Alright, Mama," I say. "Not sure how high a life-lesson can fly compared to, you know, a drone—but Merry Christmas to me, I guess."

She laughs. "Merry Christmas, indeed. You were always too smart for your britches." Her smile fades, and she leans in. "You know I love you, right? That I did this out of love?"

I don't hesitate; don't need to. But also know if I do, Mama might break. I nod and smile, then nuzzle into her. "I know, Mama. I know. And I love you, too."

I hear her sniffle once, then another time before she says, "Why don't we go make some hot chocolate and eat some of those Christmas cookies we made yesterday?"

I pull away and smile again, giving her a hug before jumping off the bed. "Alright, Mama. Let's. The day is what we make of it, right?"

"Sure thing, baby. Sure thing."

Hardest thing Ida ever had to do, sending that gift back. But there I was, sitting in the parking lot of Meyer's General, return receipt for the radio-controlled or bluetooth-controlled or whatever-the-heck-controlled green drone in one hand and a venti extra hot white mocha latte with extra whip in the other, sobbing until my windows steamed up something fierce!

But I knew deep down in my heart it was the right thing.

Spare the rod, spoil the child, the Good Book says. More like let the kid keep the cotton pickin' green drone Christmas gift he saw in Mama's closet after I told him notta and ya spoil the child.

I know the life-lesson I taught Jamal would be worth more than the drone he'd outgrow in a few months. Didn't make it any better.

Sometimes the best thing a Mama can do is return their child's Christmas gift.

Didn't make it easy, not in the slightest. But it's the long game that's important. Christmas or not.

I took a sip of my venti extra hot white mocha latte with extra whip, then another, closing my eyes as Frank Sinatra crooned on singing "Have Yourself a Merry Little Christmas."

Have yourself a merry little Christmas?

I lost it, again.

Sometimes being a parent down-right sucks. Especially during Christmas.

Then again, being a Mama is the best job in the world; yes, there's a difference. Because I get to set my son on the path of righteousness. Get to teach him what it means to be a man, even a little man, of honesty and integrity and character. Those were the better gifts, much better than a dadgum green drone!

And yet, I'm still left with the question of the day:

What to get, what to get, what to get...

I'll need another venti extra hot white mocha latte with extra whip!

Story 3

'Tis the Season

Millie had done it again. Out did herself again, more like it, rolling out one of the most inventive yet season-appropriate menu items I'd ever seen offered at Millie's on Main.

And tasted.

The turkey sausage with dried cranberry bits mixed inside was heaven. Fried on the griddle to a nice golden-brown perfection while still retaining its moisture, the salty, gamey taste of the dead bird mixing well with the tangy, tarty taste of the cranberries on top of a special blend of herbs—sage and thyme and marjoram, if I placed it right— all of it working together was something to behold.

"Well, Johnny Pope," Mille asked, standing over me while I savored every bite, "what's the verdict?"

I sat chewing, eyes closed, offering an approving grunt before washing it down with a swig of strong black coffee.

Swallowing and catching my breath, I responded, "Heaven in a sausage link, Mills. Heaven in a sausage link."

She giggled, taking out from behind her back another plate. "That's not the half of it! Check these puppies out."

I did, my eyes growing wide at the sight of three large pancakes smelling like pumpkin pie, the ground cinnamon, nutmeg, ginger, and cloves blooming from the thin, browned cakes that had a slightly orangish hue to them. But that wasn't all. For spread across them and smelling sweet and tangy was what looked like cranberry sauce, crowned with a dollop of fresh whipped cream on top.

I grinned and turned to Millie. "Doth my eyes deceive me? Is that what I think it is?"

Another giggle escaped before she explained, "Pumpkin pancakes with a cranberry compote syrup—Canadian Grade B, of course."

I smirked. "Of course! None of that hippie, low-grade Vermont Grade A crap."

She laughed that sweet, singsongy laugh of hers again, straight from the belly. "Amen to that!"

"I have to say, next Thanksgiving I'm definitely accepting Chet's invite and coming over to your house for dinner."

"That's very kind of you, Johnny, and you should have! Not sure why you didn't this year."

My smile faded. "I had some things to attend to." I left it at that.

"Well, next time then, honey." Millie tapped me on the shoulder and added, "Those pancakes and that compote are to die for. Enjoy!"

"Oh, I will," I assure her. "No doubt about that when your hand is at the breakfast-fixing wheel."

She threw up another singsongy giggle before flitting off to the next table, checking in on her diner patrons and doing her Millie thing.

I cleansed my palette with another swig of brew, then dove in.

She was right. To die for.

Finished the turkey-and-cranberry sausage links first, my tastebuds still dancing when I tackled the pumpkin pancakes. There was just enough spice, too. Not too much, not too little. More nutmeg and cloves than cinnamon, which is what pumpkin anything should be anyhow. Reminded me of Ma's Christmas pumpkin pie. She realized it shouldn't really be a thing, that late in the season and all. But Pa loved him a good homemade pumpkin pie, and after Thanksgiving she surprised him once for Christmas with another, and that was that. Pumpkin pies for Christmas until they passed this life.

A shattering broke my bliss, the crash rising above the din of diner hubbub. Didn't startle, only glanced. A decade in the private investigator gig, and then decades before that in Nam, had trained me not to react—only respond. And no response needed here. Just one of Millie's gals dropping a load all over her nice, clean black and white tiled floor. Too bad. A shame to let all those heavenly pumpkin pancakes with cranberry compote go to waste.

Speaking of which...

I returned to my own plate of heaven, finishing my final pancake and cleaning the plate.

Feeling very full, but also very satisfied that Monday morning, I leaned back in my chair at my table in the back along the set of windows facing Main Street. Tammy, another frazzled-looking server, came by with a fresh pot of brew and asked if I wanted a refill. I shoved my mug to the edge of the table and thanked her kindly.

She waddled off, and I grabbed my mug. Thought about grabbing my paper along with it, but couldn't stomach the headlines. Not after this year, these past several weeks of election crazy on top of the corona crazy. Instead, I did something I don't normally do: I sat and did nothing but stare outside at Mill Creek Junction.

The snow was really coming down now. Not surprising, giving it was nearing the end of December, and Lake Michigan was in full effect churning out the wet slush that was our state's specialty this time of year. That thick, heavy packing snow us kids would love because it meant days off from school, which would then mean the baddest, meanest snowball fights this side of the Grand River!

I took a sip, the coffee hot and heavy in my mouth, warming me as the chill seeped in through the diner's thin windows. Boy, were those the days or what? When life was simple, when life was nothing more than a snowball fight in the middle of a Michigan snow day.

The doorbell jangled, catching my attention at the front. A tall ginger with long, straight hair and a refined nose had walked in, wearing a long, tan coat past the knees doing its best to protect her bare legs. She was youngish, maybe mid-30s, holding her head high with confidence and talking with the server like she owned the joint. Probably educated, used to getting her way. Especially around working-class folk like Tammy trying to find her a seat.

As a PI, I was prone to take in such pedestrian details as coat lengths and bare legs and levels of social and educational standing. Even the crimson hair clip at the back of her head. Not red, not purple. Crimson. She was a looker, that's for sure. If I was half my age, I'd make up an excuse to walk her way. Maybe drop something at her feet or stumble along the way.

I took another swig of coffee as the woman was seated a few booths down from me on the other side of the aisle. She took off her coat, revealing a tight-fitting black dress and a chunky gold necklace. Didn't recognize her. Then again, I didn't recognize many of the youngsters that had felt called to call the Junction their home.

A thought overtook me as I sat nursing my coffee. Sudden and invasive. Accosted me really, as I didn't see it coming. Not in the slightest.

Could be her...

I leaned back in my seat, downing the rest of the lukewarm brew and setting the mug down on the table with a smack.

Could be.

I swallowed hard and looked out the window again, the snow continuing its relentless assault on Mill Creek, the dawning light casting a foreboding gray across Main Street I didn't like. Especially since my subconscious decided to bring up that nugget to chew on for God only knew what reason.

Because by *her*, my prefrontal cortex was trying to get me to think about the daughter I left behind when Lynn passed giving birth. Truth be told, it's why I got into the PI gig to begin with. And the priesthood gig. The latter to atone for my sins of abandoning our daughter at that firehouse after Lynn gave birth and passed; the former trying to hunt her down after all these years after abandoning her at the firehouse.

I reached for my mug again to take another swig and swat away the synaptic tricks my brain was playing with me. Only I realized I'd drained the thing dry.

Damn prefrontal, putting those damn ideas in my head at a time like this. At Christmas! Pretty much came around like clockwork this time of year, that longing for the one remaining connection to family left in the world after Lynn passed. The longing for that one remaining connection to Lynn that was left in the world...

Or maybe it was the Holy Spirit, throwing up a signal flare to get my attention. Suggesting that maybe she was the one, or at least she was still out there.

Tammy swung by and refilled the mug, startling me from my deep thoughts. I smiled and thanked her, then she hustled off to the next table. I went to take another swig when the door jangled again at the front.

Another woman with a long overcoat entered, off-white this time. Her hair silver and cut at the ears and styled big. She was older than the last, but carried herself in the same manner, sporting the same refined nose and eyes.

My heart skipped a beat before my stomach sank to the black and white tiled floor.

I'd recognize that nose anywhere, and hair. Had history with both.

The woman scanned the place looking for someone, the chunky gold necklace from the first broad replaced by a string of large pearls and complementary earrings. Smiling, she darted my way.

I stood, forcing a grin to play across my face and arms widening for the embrace I knew would be coming from a woman I hadn't seen in years, a decade even, but had a past that stretched well past that.

That dame Elizabeth Nolland.

"Liddy..." I crooned, mouth wide with delight, arms still wide with a bit of hopeful expectation.

Elizabeth rounded the row of booths stretching down my aisle and stopped short. She startled at first, not registering what her eyes were glimpsing. Then she clutched her chest with dramatic flare, gasping and grinning in a show that was particularly pleasing.

And in that mis-planted Tennessean drawl that melted

my heart since the '80s, she crooned back, "Jonathan Papadopulos, as I live and breathe!"

Liddy trotted over and returned the embrace, placing a peck on my right cheek that warmed me more than Millie's pumpkin pancakes and coffee.

She stepped back with a wide smile. "It's been ages, darling. So good to see you! What have you been up to?"

"Oh, you know. A little of this, a little of that."

A little of this, a little of that? Get it together, JP! You sound like a used car salesman, for crying out loud.

"Well, last I heard you were a priest at Saint Thomas's up the road."

I smiled. "Yes, well, not since about a decade ago, but, yes—" I continued stammering before taking a breath. "You're right. That's true, I was."

I swallowed hard, wishing Tammy would have brought me a glass of water to go along with that refill of brew.

"Loved that about you. Doing the Lord's work, you were."

"You as well, Liddy. Stewarding the Fourth Estate to keep these Junction jokers in line."

She startled, swallowing and glancing behind her. "Fourth Estate, you say?"

A brief furrow fluttered across my brow in confusion. "Yeah, you know, the Fourth Estate. The press and news media, keeping the other three knucklehead branches of government in line. Especially the three Junction branches in the courts and council and mayor's office."

She giggled nervously, glancing behind her again, before clutching her chest and then letting out a laugh. "Yes, well, all that's in the past now."

I brushed off the weird exchange and crossed my arms, then leaned in. "So I heard..."

It was quite the talk of town that the baroness of the only newspaper in town, the *Mill Creek Junction Guardian*, had handed over the reins to her granddaughter, Tracy Nolland. Always thought the name was a bit pretentious. Wasn't there some daily Brit rag across the pond called *The Guardian?* Name was shooting way above the Junction's status in the world, as if the Nollands themselves were standing athwart the forces seeking to bring Mill Creek to its knees.

At any rate, Tracy's first duty had been to expose the Mayor for trying to leverage the Prosecuting Attorney's office to sully the reputation of his only election competition in ages, the city councilwoman Claudia Pentwell. That went over real well, with both the mayor and his beloved citizenry. But the kid had to make a splash, I got that. Especially with the way small-town newspapers were going these days with the world's move online and social media. Glancing over Liddy's shoulder now at the younger broad sitting uncomfortably at the booth behind her, I wondered if that was her.

She giggled again. "Speaking of which..." She turned around to the booth where the woman I had first seen come in sat, motioning for her to stand. "Come along, dear. Now, this is my granddaughter, Tracy."

I smiled and nodded toward the young woman, who eased out from the booth and stood. "I thought she looked familiar. A spitting image of her illustrious, exquisite, beautiful beyond—"

"Oh, stop, Jonathan!" Liddy said with a giggle, batting at me with her hand in a way that told me to keep going. "Tracy, meet Jonathan Papadopoulos. He and I go way back."

She turned back to me with a wry grin playing across her lips, adding, "Don't we, dear?"

I felt heat rising at the back of my neck, and I prayed to the Lord Almighty that my cheeks weren't growing as red as they felt.

"I'm sorry," Liddy continued, "what is it you do nowadays, dear?"

"Private—" My throat caught on my dry tongue. I swallowed and continued, "I'm a private investigator, Liddy."

"A PI?" Her eyes got big, and she turned toward Tracy. "How about that?"

"And you must be the very capable woman," I said to Tracy, "whom the venerable Liddy Nolland is turning over the reins to her gazette."

Liddy turned to me and frowned. "*Guardian*, Jonathan. *Guardian*! How many times do I have to tell you?"

I chuckled. "Yeah, yeah. So, handing over the deed to the family business, are you, Liddy?" I leaned in with a serious face. "Has she been properly vetted?"

Liddy laughed. "Why, are you offering your services?"

"I'm always at your service." I took a bow, then went on, "A friend in need is a friend indeed, as the saying goes."

"Hold on." It was Tracy. She continued, "You're a private investigator, is that right?"

"That's right."

"Are you, like, licensed and credentialed?"

"As licensed and credentialed as the great State of Michigan requires."

"Any professional acquaintances?"

This was odd. Felt like the conversation suddenly shifted into a job interview. Perhaps that was simply the reporter head of hers.

"Not sure you would call Gideon O'Donnell all that

professional, but I ply my services in his neck of the Junction woods." That got a knowing laugh from the ladies. "As well as for others. Why do you ask?"

She glanced at her grandmother, who glanced my way and smiled, as if the pair were in on something.

Liddy said, "Would you mind joining us, Jonathan?" She motioned toward the booth where Tracy had been seated.

I nodded and joined them, intrigued but also growing concerned my day had just taken a turn.

The pair said nothing for several seconds, shifting in their seats and looking over their shoulders.

"Liddy, you're making me nervous," I finally said. "Like we're about to break wide open some Junctiongate, or something."

She laughed quietly. "No, it's nothing like that."

"Then what is it like?"

She took a breath. Then she leaned in and whispered, "Well, it's just that we've got a situation on our hands. And you might be the person who could help."

"What kind of situation?"

Liddy hesitated, leaning back and handing over the reins to Tracy.

"Somebody is stalking us," she said.

I raised a brow. "Stalking?"

"That may not be the correct work."

"Threatening, more like it," Liddy added.

Now I was worried. "How so?"

"We, each of us," Tracy said, pointing to her grandmother, "have received several letters the past several weeks."

"At first," Liddy added, "they were simply angry missives about the direction of the *Guardian*. Nothing we haven't received from the great citizens of Mill Creek Junction stretching back through the century to our founding."

Tracy said, "But also unlike anything we've received before."

"How so?" I asked.

"We'll get to that, but initially we sort of just shrugged them off. Like Grandma said, we get angry letters all the time. But over the past few weeks, they've gotten worse. More threatening, violent even.

Alarm bells were going off now. "Violent, you say?"

"Nothing specific, mind you," Liddy whispered. "Only vague references to us being sorry and paying for our mistakes and missteps."

"What has Mill Creek PD said about it all? This is catnip for Chief Roller. Surely he's all over this thing."

Liddy looked at Tracy and frowned. Tracy leaned in and whispered, "We haven't gone to the police yet."

My eyes got big again. "What? Why not? Seems like a pretty big deal, if what you say is true, that your lives are being threatened by some crazy reader."

"That's why we were meeting. To discuss next steps."

"And there you were," Liddy said, smiling now. "Standing in the middle of Millie's on Main. An angel PI sent from heaven!"

I smiled and bowed my head with embarrassment, that heat returning to the back of my neck. "Now, I don't know about that..."

"We could really use a private investigator on this to keep it private. Could really use your help specifically, Jonathan, knowing you and your character."

"But why? Why keep it from the police, why keep it private?"

Tracy answered, "Because we're pretty sure we know who it is."

"And who's that?"

Tracy looked at her grandmother. Liddy nodded her forward.

"James Fitzgerald," she revealed.

My eyes widened. "The former editor-in-chief of the *Mill Creek Junction Guardian?*"

She nodded. "That's right."

"Unfortunately," Liddy said, stepping in, "it appears the man who has been mailing our offices and my home these disturbing letters."

"*Threatening* letters," Tracy added, putting a hand to Liddy's back as she brought a hand to her mouth, sounding like she was choking up. She smiled at her granddaughter at the gesture and put a hand on her leg.

This was unreal. James Fitzgerald, sending disturbing, threatening letters to the Nollands? The man and his family were part of my Saint Thomas parish back in the day, when he and they were younger. A year into marriage with a newborn, if I recall. The man had been a pillar of the community, rising through the *Guardian* to chief, until he was replaced months ago by Tracy, Liddy's granddaughter. Understandably wanted to pass the business along to her family, with them in charge. Didn't hear much of anything surrounding the transfer of power, so to speak. And now to hear James was some sort of Son of Sam in the making?

"Why on earth do you think it's him?" I finally said. "Does not compute. Not with what I know of the man."

Trace reached in a handbag she had set next to her in the booth and pulled out a cream folder. She set it on the table and pushed it across to me.

I eyed her before picking it up and opening it. Inside

were a number of white pieces of copy paper with cut-out pieces of newspapers and magazines and Sunday advertisements. I thumbed through the sheets, counting ten or twelve, all sporting the same cut-out letters and sentences, in various colors and fonts, spelling out his demands and threats.

I looked from Tracy to Liddy and said, "Is this for real? These are from your guy?"

Liddy nodded, face drawn and serious now. "As you can see, we've received several of these missives from James."

I scoffed. "This is Perry Mason level criminal conspiracy here if James is threatening you with cut-outs from newspapers."

"*Our* newspaper."

I chuckled. "Even better! And if it's him, these are from *his* newspaper by his view of things, I'd wager."

"Exactly!" Tracy said. "That's what makes the whole thing so creepy."

"It also doesn't make him a stalker or murderer in the making."

"This does." She leaned over and pointed at the top sheet, to a line toward the end. It read: '*The newspaper is a greater treasure to the people than uncounted millions of gold. And James Fitzgerald was its chief miner! Bring him back to the Fourth Estate, or else.*'

"What's that about?"

"It's from Henry Ward Beecher. A minister from the 19th century and founder and editor of a newspaper in New York."

"Sounds like Harriet Beacher Stow, author of *Uncle Tom's Cabin*. Any relation?"

"Brother and sister."

"That quotation Tracy pointed to there," Liddy

explained, "was a trademark of James. Would open every one of our team meetings with it, reminding the crew of their important duty to the good people of Mill Creek Junction."

Tracy added, "And he would constantly refer to the *Guardian* as the Junction's Fourth Estate, holding the courts', the council's, and the mayor's feet to the fire."

"Which is why," I said, "you flinched when I mentioned the Fourth Estate."

Liddy smirked. "Was it that obvious?"

"Not really. But I'm a PI, remember?"

"Oh, Jonathan," she moaned, "what are we to do? Tracy and I aren't too keen on getting the police involved. Not yet anyway."

"Why not? Seems like something Chief Roller should be brought into, especially if there's been a threat of violence." I leaned in closer, adding lowly, "Has there been?"

"Not directly," Tracy said. "Not yet, anyway. Just the vague 'or else' and 'you'll be sorry' missives."

"Do you think he's capable of carrying through with it?"

She took a breath, looking to Liddy.

Liddy answered, "I cannot imagine it! I have known the man for thirty years. I have to believe these are the ravings of a broken man. Something must have happened to trigger him so."

"Trigger? How long ago did these start arriving?"

"A month ago," Tracy said, "just after the election."

I asked, "Do you think your coverage of the mayor triggered it?"

She shrugged. "Who knows? But they've been pretty steady ever since. Mailed to Grandma's home address and my direct mail at the office, which James definitely would have known about."

I considered this, wondering, worrying. None of it sat right, and I sure as heck wasn't in the mood that morning to get into a high-stakes conspiracy to snuff out the *Guardian's* owner and editor-in-chief.

But it was Liddy, and her granddaughter. Not sure how I could say no.

"Again, why not go to the police?" I asked.

"We would rather settle this quietly," Tracy said, "given the relationship between James and the Nolland family. We also would like to avoid the optics for the *Guardian*."

"Being what business is with newspapers nowadays."
She nodded.

I took a breath, taking this all in. "Why me?"

"Because I trust you, Jonathan," Liddy said, fixing me with those deep pools of blue that I have always appreciated.

She did too. I could tell by the look in her eyes. I also saw desperation, and fear. Neither of which I ever wanted to see in those pools of blue.

So I said, "Alright. I'll help."

Those eyes brightened back up to before this whole blasted conversation started.

"Oh, goodie," Liddy said, mouth wide and color returning to her face.

"Thank you, Mr. Papadopoulos. I—" Tracy gestured to her grandmother, "we appreciate it."

"Johnny Pope, is fine. And I'm happy to help. Are there any others you have in mind?"

Tracy took out her phone. "I'll send you the list of people we've compiled, but we're pretty sure it's James."

I gave her my phone number, then received a text with an attachment.

"If you find anything, be gentle, Jonathan," Liddy said. "James was a dear soul, and I sorrowed so having to let him go. But the *Guardian* needed new direction, needed new blood. Be gentle, and tell him we forgive him. 'Tis the season, after all."

I nodded and slid out from the booth, having all I needed to get to work. "I understand. I'll deliver the appropriate message for the circumstances. The appropriate *gentle* message."

"Along with our forgiveness."

I found that an interesting request, something Liddy was clearly interested in. Here was a lady whose life was being threatened, and she wanted to make sure she forgave the perp? What a dame.

I nodded. She reached for my hand resting on the table and gave it a squeeze, mouthing *'Thank you!'* I nodded again, then headed back home to get to work as the lunch crowd started in.

Didn't have many hours in the day left, and I'd need all I could to get a jump on a situation that was beyond my pay grade. Thought about heading straight to MCPD and having an off-the-record chit-chat with Chief Roller, but I knew Liddy wouldn't have liked that. I could appreciate her wanting discretion with this one, given the relationship she'd had with James and the unwanted press it would garner—which was ironic, since they were the only press in town! Either way, I went straight home and got to work.

Snow had abated some, fluttering to the ground now in fits and starts. Throwing a few logs on bunched up newspaper in my fireplace, I struck up a match and set the pile on fire. Flames chewed instantly through the paper and set the dry wood ablaze. I poured myself a glass of fifteen-year-old Glenfiddich, neat of course, then grabbed my MacBook and sat in an overstuffed leather chair that had become my office.

Now I was ready to go.

Tools of the trade nowadays for gigs like this would put Magnum P.I. to shame. A MacBook and a subscription to TruthHunter did a world of good sussing out the details of people's lives they'd rather keep private. Except nothing was private nowadays, not with the way criminal backgrounds are public record and people's social media accounts are crawlable by bots. Even financial records aren't fool-proof private—if you're good and know where to look.

I'm good and know where to look.

So I did.

First thing I saw was the pages James Fitzgerald liked on the WeShare social media platform. Second Amendment stuff, prepper groups, citizen militias, even some anti-government types. None of it together added up to anything, except he hadn't liked the *Guardian's* social media page. Which made sense, since he'd been sacked. Again, wasn't causation, not even all that correlative, but it was interesting.

Other thing I saw was that the guy was in debt up to his eyeballs. House was double mortgaged. Two existing car loans totaling six-figures. Two kids in four-year colleges milking non-adulting adulting for all its worth while bleeding Dad dry. Reason enough to become unhinged after losing a cushy job at the top of the *Guardian* that was paying all this down.

Kept going down the rabbit trail and saw he had a conceal-carry weapon permit, which made me a little nervous. Had a record of petty assault, which was surprising. Just a few weeks ago. Apparently James got into it with his neighbor when his candidate lost, and he went through the man's yard tearing out the political signs for the guy who did win. Didn't get any time, paid a fine, promised to be a good boy. Again, no causation, but maybe correlation with the weird notes being sent Liddy's and Tracy's way.

Alright, enough hemming and hawing, time to get down to business. Had plenty to go on and enough to put me over the edge. James Fitzgerald was plausible enough to fit the bill. And in my world, plausible meant as much as probable. A trip to the man's house for a look-see and a nice low-key, friendly chat would do the trick.

But man...last thing I wanted to do a week before Christmas. Although, with the guy threatening Liddy, and in the way he was doing the threatening—would take a regular Nor'easter skimming across New York and Pennsylvania on west across Lake Ontario and pummeling West Michigan with two feet of snow before I'd let a hair on that dame's head get touched by the likes of Fitzgerald.

So I grabbed a stocking cap, white not black. No need to give the wrong impression when I strolled up on the guy. I left the scarf and gloves, not figuring they were necessary. Then I walked out to my vintage Ford F-150 and climbed in. Heading down Main Street on toward Old Town Junction, I was glad I sprang for those upper-level Bridgestones at the rate the snow was falling. We might get that two feet yet!

It was just after dinner when I arrived at Fitzgerald's house, a nice two-story white Victorian thing with black trim and two tall Corinthian columns holding up a walk-out porch on the second floor. Leftover from the Junction's early founding, if I recall.

Candles were lit in the windows, their little yellow

lights haloing against the window. A large wreath hung above the front door, large red bulbs arrayed around its woven pine branches and lit up by white Christmas lights. The smell of burning wood in a fireplace nearby wafted inside my cabin, all cedary and spicy and reminding me of nights curled up with Lynn in the '70s with a bottle of wine in front of a roaring fire in our split-level south of Main. I breathed in deep and closed my eyes, those memories etched in my very soul. Sweet, but distracting.

Shaking them off, I rolled up my window and shut off the Ford, getting ready to rumble.

Fireplace was maybe Fitzgerald's. No, probably Fitzgerald's. Using it to burn the remains of his newspapers, if I were him. Hiding the evidence and all. Although his type wasn't that savvy. Probably kept the remains in the front closet with the firewood to use as a starter when the days grew longer and turned bitter, more toward late-January, early February. Better yet, probably just threw them out with the morning trash.

Enough of this hemming and hawing. Time to get to it.

Opening the door, I stepped out into the December evening, the crisp air slapping me in the face and making me regret not bringing my scarf and gloves. But that cedary, spicy smoke drifted back my way on a light breeze, warming me and carrying me across the road to the target.

Still couldn't wrap my mind around it, though. James Fitzgerald, leaving threatening notes demanding the former editor-in-chief's reinstatement—his reinstatement? Did not compute. Like something out of some bargain-bin Kindle mystery yarn. It made no sense!

Especially since the guy had been one of my parishioners at Saint Thomas. Just couldn't wrap my mind around him threatening a septuagenarian and her thirtysomething granddaughter that way. Especially in such an obvious way. I mean, how many *Guardian* readers were that invested in the guy's editorial suggestions and publishing decisions to demand that he be reinstated, or they would come after Liddy and Tracy?

Again, like something out of some bargain-bin Kindle mystery yarn. It was preposterous!

Then again, I suppose you never really know a guy. Especially when he's down on his luck, and during the holidays. No job at his age, with a wife and kids, and a mortgage, presents to buy and dinners to host—I suppose a man might do a lot of crazy things if he thought it would do him any good, if it would get him his job back.

Like sending threatening notes written in newspaper cut-outs demanding the former editor-in-chief be reinstated.

Then again, a second time, I just couldn't make sense of it. Suppose time would tell...

And sooner than later.

I reached Fitzgerald's walkway leading straight to that massive wreath all lit up over his front door.

Until I saw a trash can parked out at the curb. Not one of those old-school metal things with the massive circular top and handle. The new-school blue ones. More an oversized garbage can. Plasticy and big and perfect for hiding someone's newfound extracurricular activity cutting out threatening anti-Dear Johns and sending them to former places of employ.

So I hoofed it over for a little look-see.

Glancing a round, my breath billowing behind me in the frigid December evening air, I opened the top and eased it back on easy hinges. The beauty of plastic garbage containers. Back in the day, I'd have been worried about those dang aluminum cans throwing up all kinds of noise. Nope, not these. Easy peasy.

I reached inside and frowned, pulling out a stack of newspapers.

There they were. A variety of Sunday spreads and grocery-store weeklies. Looked like Swiss cheese they were missing so many of their letters. Upper and lower cases. The paper and toner pretty well matching what I had been given in that cream folder.

As I said, his type ain't that savvy.

I shook my head and stuffed them under my arm, carrying them back to my truck and depositing them in the passenger's seat. Then I hoofed it over to Fitzgerald's front door and knocked. Rule of thumb was to get straight to the point. No need to pussyfoot when people's lives were on the line.

Took a minute, but soon there was a rattling at the door and it cracked open. An eye appeared, then widened before the door opened even wider and James was standing in front of me, hair thin and overgrown, face gaunt and tired, clothes rumpled and Blue Light Special variety. Not a good look for a man who had spent his life in a suit and tie and pocket square, hair trimmed and slick and feasting on the best slabs of beef and bottles of wine Mill Creek could muster.

"Uh, hey, Johnny!" Fitzgerald stammered. "How—how you doing?"

I smiled, cupping my hands in front of me, all casual like. "Oh, I'm fine. Was in the neighborhood and thought I'd stop by. Thought I'd say howdy."

"Uh, great! Thanks..."

I could tell the guy was totally thrown. Had hardly exchanged two words with one another over the years since

I left Saint Thomas. Even then, he hadn't come much in those latter years anyway. Mostly the Easter and Christmas type, except for his wife and kids who were regulars. Now I'm stopping by to say howdy? Please!

"Can I come in?" I asked.

"Uh, OK...but why?"

Dang. Thought I had him. So I improvised. "Need a bathroom." I did a little dance and smiled again. "Real bad."

"Oh, sure!" He opened the door and let me in. Midwest manners never failed in these parts.

I walked into a nicely appointed living room. Baby grand, chase lounger, hardwood floors, navy blue walls with white crown molding running around the room, a fire blazing away in a black marble fireplace. Beyond was a large formal dining room in cherry furniture, shrouded in darkness, then a kitchen with the lights on over a granite island.

Nothing out of the ordinal on my quick assessment.

Except one thing.

"Where's Mary and the kids?" I asked.

"Uh..." he said, looking around. Which seemed to be his standard response. "Out?"

I nodded, frowning with contemplation.

"Mall," he added, as if he needed to define what 'Out' meant. But the one-word answers were annoying, and odd.

"Ahh, of course," I said. "So...about that bathroom?"

"Right. Down the hall to the right, then hang another right. Can't miss it."

"Thanks! I'll be just a minute."

"Care for a drink when you come back?" he said.

Don't mind if I do...

"Sure. A beer or whiskey would be great."

"I'll grab something. Be back in a jiff."

He left while I wandered down the hallway he pointed

past the baby grand, the walls lined with pictures of his family. Wife and two boys.

Glancing behind, I caught him heading toward the kitchen. I kept going, snagging a left where I knew a study sat from a floor plan I had found on Zillow. Door was closed, and when I went to turn the knob, I discovered it was locked as well.

Of course. Locked study.

Padding back down the hall, I checked to see if James had returned.

Not yet, some clangs echoing down from the kitchen. A matter of minutes until he returned with those drinks.

So I got to work, pulling out a sleeve of lock picks from my back pocket. Clutching the study doorknob, I worked the pick until I heard a soft *click*.

I turned the knob, opened the door, and stepped inside.

Then dropped my jaw.

Mary, mother of God...

It was dark, but the light coming from the room behind was all I needed to see the room plastered with newspaper clippings and photos—of Tracy and Liddy, of their homes and them their cars, of them walking on the street or eating at a restaurant. There were things drawn on them and string running from one to the other. It was like something out of a bad *Law and Order* episode.

And way worse than I could have possibly imagined.

Before I could really react to what I was seeing, there was the soft clink of tumblers or bottles from behind.

Then: "I'm screwed, aren't I."

I took a breath before doing anything. Didn't spin to face Fitzgerald. Nothing sudden, nothing alarming.

Instead, I eased around one foot. There he was, holding two beer bottles and looking more sad than anything. He was lumpy and definitely out of shape. Larger than me, but I knew I could take him if I needed to.

He didn't do anything, but I didn't put it past him to take me on. Especially with what I saw behind me. What he knew I had seen. A man will do anything to preserve what little life he has left.

The silence began to stretch, so I filled it: "Libby and Tracy Nolland sent me. They know, James."

A sigh escaped the man, like a tire deflating. Then he stumbled back into the living room, setting the drinks on a marble-top table and slumping into the chase lounger.

Time to end this, once and for all.

I walked toward him. "Talk to me, James. What happened? What's this about?"

He snapped his head toward me, eyes narrowing and growing with fire. "What happened? I'm sure you know very well what happened. I was fired!"

I put out a staying hand. "I understand the *Guardian* made some changes. Heck, I've been there myself once or twice, canned and down on my luck. But sending threatening letters?" I sat on the baby grand's bench, continuing, "That's not you, James. What's this about?"

"My life is over! Don't you understand? My job was everything to me. Everything! And now Mary's left and taken the boys. There's nothing. I have nothing. I *am* nothing!"

He took one of the bottles and chugged back the beer. Several gulps until it was half gone. He set it back down on the marble hard with an echoey clang. Then he buried his head in his hands, muffled whimpers floating around the room in a mournful dirge.

James was right. He was done. At least, he thought he was. Lost his job, lost his family, lost his life. And all right before the holiday season, before Christmas even. The perfect image of small-town America had crumbled around him, and he was left in the middle of the pile with the pieces scattered about. Would make many men go bonkers. Even to the point of lashing out with threatening letters written using cut-up newspapers and advertisers.

I cleared my throat, getting down to business. "The Nollands have instructed me to share with you their intent not to bring this matter to the police. Neither do they intend to prosecute you for the threats against their lives."

He looked up but didn't move, didn't say a word.

"They understand," I continued, "the tremendous stress you must be under, given the circumstances of the holiday season and trying to find a new job. They just want the harassment to stop. Do you understand?"

His face fell now, but he nodded.

"They also forgive you."

Moisture sprang to James's eyes, and it looked like the weight of the world had just rolled off his shoulders.

"Forgive me?" he asked on a disbelieving breath.

I nodded. "Forgive you."

He furrowed his brow and shook his head. "But why? I understand what I did. I really do."

"Good. Then you know it has to stop."

My voice was hard and firm and no-nonsense. He had to know who he was dealing with. It wasn't just Liddy and Tracy anymore. It was me.

He nodded quickly. "I understand. It was a stupid thing to do, threatening them and all."

I snorted a laugh. "You could say that again. And throwing in your favorite Stow quote wasn't the wisest move. '*The newspaper is a greater treasure to the people than uncounted millions of gold.*' A dead giveaway."

His face fell, as if he was punched in the gut by his own hand. James cleared his throat. "You didn't answer me."

"Oh, yeah? And what's that?"

"Why are they forgiving me?"

I shrugged. "'Tis the season, I suppose."

He nodded and hung his head.

"But it's probably more than that," I added, never one to waste a moment to sermonize.

He raised his head now. "It is?"

"It's like the Gospel writer wrote, John the Apostle. *'The true light that gives light to everyone was coming into the world. He was in the world, and though the world was made through him, the world did not recognize him. He came to that which was his own, but his own did not receive him. Yet to all who did receive him, to those who believed in his name, he gave the right to become children of God—children born not of natural descent, nor of human decision or a husband's will, but born of God.'"*

The man furrowed his brow and nodded, as if trying to contemplate my meaning but looking like he wasn't getting there.

So I helped him along. "Here's where the rubber meets the road. Jesus, the True Light, was born to save a world who rejected him, the God and Creator of the world. Not only that, he was born into a nation to save them, the Messiah who would finally set things right. Yet Israel rejected him, to the point of nailing him to a cross."

"And, what, you're saying Elizabeth Nolland is the Messiah? My Messiah?"

I could tell the man's temperature was being ratcheted up now. He was getting hotter than I wanted. Definitely not what I needed.

I chuckled. "She may think so, but no."

He offered a chuckle of his own, deflating the tension a bit.

"What I mean is, even though Jesus was rejected by the world, by his own people, he died for them, forgave them, saved them even. If I know Liddy Nolland as well as I think I do, I know that truth sits at the heart of her very own soul. You rejected her, wanted her dead even. Yet she doesn't want the same ill for you. She still cares about you, loves you even."

That seemed to steal his breath. He grabbed that half-drained bottle and chugged the rest, then slumped back in the lounger.

"Understand what I'm driving at? You reject her, she receives you. Doesn't make sense, but it's the way of love. The way of Liddy Nolland. The way of the Christmas season."

He offered a weak smile and nodded, whispering, "Understand."

I stood, so did he. Then he extended his hand. "Always did enjoy your homilies, Father."

I grabbed it and shook it. "Not Father anymore, Mr. Fitzgerald. But I appreciate the compliment just the same."

The man went to pull away, but I wouldn't let him. "We're good, right? We have an understanding? No more threats, no more letters. And you're absolved of your transgressions and got Liddy's forgiveness and love? She's not going to the police and you're dropping this—" I pulled him in closer, adding: "Now."

Felt a little bad ending things that way. But given the stakes—not just the threats on the Nolland ladies' lives, but the threat to Liddy in particular—I needed to have our understanding voiced one final time.

James's eyes went wide, and he nodded five quick nods.

Probably as surprised by his former priest tightening the screws one final time as he was that he would be asked.

But the man confirmed what I needed. "Yes, we're good. I understand."

I grinned. "Great, Mr. Fitzgerald. You have yourself a merry little Christmas, you hear?"

"You too, Fath—I mean, Johnny."

I let go and turned toward the front door, then heard the man's throat clear behind me.

"Johnny," Fitzgerald said. "Could you do one thing for me?"

I stopped, clenching my jaw and figuring what was coming next. But turned around for it anyway.

"Yes, James. What can I do you for?"

"Will you..." He paused, mustering up the courage. Then he stood stiffly and went for it: "Will you hear my confession?"

Funny thing about this gig as a PI on the other side of the priesthood. This happened more often than not with the perps I chased.

So I did what I always did. I listened, I absolved, I extended Christ's forgiveness.

'Tis the season, I suppose.

Ring in the Season

Mill Creek Junction was the last place on God's green earth I'd ever imagined myself waking up on a weekend in a turn-of-the-century, two-story craftsman bungalow the winter after turning 40. Me, Gideon O'Donnell!

Yet there I was, Alexa speaking sweet nothings into my REM morning dreams, beckoning me to seize the day while the warming scent of coffee set to auto-brew wafted through my house and the dawning day peaked through my darkening shades.

I told Alexa to shove it where the sun doesn't shine, turning to my side and throwing my heavy down-feather duvet back over my head. Until I remembered what day it was.

Ring shopping day!

Or rather, jewelry browsing day with the intention of learning Annabelle Kirkland's finger size and diamond preference and all the other myriad of other pre-engagement things a guy needs to know before he pops the question. An outing she didn't know the true intention, and a question she didn't know was coming, though would expect it—and hopefully welcome it!

I threw off the covers and slid out of bed, my feet settling onto the hardwood floor that was surprisingly warm and ready to do what Alexa was inviting me to do.

First things first....

I crept to my window to check out the damage from the night's snowstorm. AccuWeather was promising a load of lake effect snow across West Michigan. Peeling back those room-darkening shades, I discovered a winter wonderland outside. The app more than delivered!

Snow was falling just right, the big, chunky snow flakes descending like Norman Rockwell himself had summoned them for a portrait of small-town America. A blanket of sculpted white stuff draped the hedgerow between the next-door neighbor and a foot of the same spread out across the back lawn like a frosted sheet cake. The century-old oaks dotting my backyard held more of the same with pride, like it was their duty while naked of leaves.

My mouth curled upward at the sight. "Last place on God's green earth, is right..."

Which was fine by me, especially because I was fixing to propose to a Junction gal I'd been dating for all of four months. Not a local gal, mind you; she was from the South. Not Deep South, but definitely not from the Midwest; Tennessee was far enough as far could get without messing with one's DNA. Still, she was the local assistant prosecuting attorney, which was enough local to set my mind fluttering and my subconscious flaring up all kinds of signals second guessing and are-you-sureing—enough to get a guy doing all the above and more!

But I knew it deep in my bones she was the one for me. And that day was the day I'd make it all happen.

I set the darkening blinds back into place and slid my feet into some leather slippers before throwing on a blue terry-cloth robe Ma got me for Christmas last year. Then I sauntered downstairs for that coffee filling up the house with its sweet-smelling nectar.

Sauntering down the stairs, my footfalls echoing with too much *clomp* for early morning, I returned to my REM-dream-state ruminating. The one about never imagining picturing myself a Mill Creek Junction lifer—knowing it was more than pre-game, pre-engagement jitters.

Never in my wildest imaginations did I picture myself practicing law back in my small-town hometown. Corporate gigs were where it was at. Any first year knew that. And every Georgetown University student worth his salt knew they were destined to greatness in one of the big urban centers of law.

DC, LA, NY.

The top three letter combos were high on my list. Followed by Atlanta, Houston, and Chicago. Maybe Detroit, but it was a bit close to home. And they got worse winters than us Junction folks.

So practicing law in MCJ? Definitely not!

I smiled again, and took a swig of coffee, the burnt beans adequately masked by cream and sugar, feeling like I'd made the best decision ever moving back home to set up my small-town law practice. Mill Creek Junction never looked so good. Mostly because I was getting ready to make the biggest decision of my life—the size and style of the ring that would go on the finger of the woman I wanted to marry.

A purring *pring-pring-pring* flared up from my cell phone still resting on its charger at a desk behind me in front of the marble-top island. Never brought that thing to bed with me; too distracting.

Taking another swig, I walked over to the desk and snatched up the phone. The area code was 616, so it was local, but I didn't recognize the number.

I answered it anyway. "Hello?"

"Gideon O'Donnell?"

"This is him."

"It's Herb Landry."

My mouth widened into another grin. I was hoping he would call. The man himself from Landry Jewelers.

But then it fell. Was there a problem? Did he need to cancel?

"Mr. O'Donnell, are you there?" the man asked, voice old and gentle and refined.

I cleared my throat. "Yes—Yes, Mr. Landry. Sorry. Is there a problem?"

"Oh, no problem at all. Just making sure we were on for our afternoon appointment. I've arranged a special selection of diamonds in all carrots and cuts and clarity."

"Carrots and cuts and clarity?"

"Yes...the three Cs of diamonds."

I chuckled. "I'm aware, Mr. Landry. I didn't expect the afternoon to be so...involved."

Now he chuckled. "But of course it's *involved*. You're shopping for a blooming engagement ring!"

"I suppose so."

"Then I shall expect you at 1:30 p.m., then?"

"Sharp."

The man hummed, and I imagined the ends of his mouth curling upward even as he imagined dollar signs dancing in his head like sugarplums.

"Excellent, Mr. O'Donnell. See you then!"

We hung up, those three Cs flashing before my eyes again, along with my own visions of dollar signs. Then I went back to my coffee, glancing outside at the snow really picking up now as I drained my coffee. I was going to need it.

I showered before making myself a plate of scrambled eggs with cheese and raspberry-jellied toast. I poured myself another cup of coffee and sat down with my iPad and the *New York Times* app—

When my phone flared up another *pring-pring-pring* purr. This time I recognized the number.

"Hey there, babe. Ready for our fun-filled afternoon?"

All I got was an earful of nose blowing. "Hey, yourself."

I frowned, holding the phone away from my ear it filled with another bout of blowing. I shuddered at it all, feeling like the germs were oozing through my cell phone. Felt the urge to reach for the travel hand sanitizer and wipe down the thing it was so disgusting! But I held firm, reaching for one of those round squeeze balls I keep handy whenever my germaphobia flares up.

"You there, darlin'?" Annabelle asked, sounding like she was talking through a fish tank. Judging by the amount of snot she just blew, that pretty well fit the bill!

"Yeah, babe, but you sound awful."

She cleared her throat, and I braced for another round of blowing. "No, I'm fine. Really. Just the sniffles."

"Sounds like more than the sniffles!" Then it hit me, and I sucked in a startled breath. "You don't think—"

"Stop! I'm fine. It's just a cold. Are we still on for coffee? Although, Lord only knows why we can't just have a cup at your place," she mumbled before another blow.

I winced, but smiled. I hadn't told her about the ring shopping date. Only to meet at Starbucks for coffee. Plan was to go for a stroll and just happen by Landry's Jewelers, then go inside for a look-see. Didn't plan on the snow dump, or the cold.

"You sure you're still up for it?" I asked.

"Pish posh! I'm ready to go tobogganing if it comes to it."

I chuckled. "Alright, then. So Starbucks at one?"

"Starbucks at one. See you then, darlin'." She gave one more blow for good measure before hanging up.

I took in a measured breath, feeling slightly bad I was dragging her out into the winter wonderland. Should be bringing her chicken noodle soup, not ring shopping. But I was pretty pumped to get the final piece to pop the question.

Just hoped I didn't make things worse!

Walked the few blocks from my house down to Main Street, hanging a left down toward the Starbucks next to my law office—although I preferred independently owned coffee shops, something Annabelle and I shared. Used to have more of a local vibe, having been owned by Mayor Goodall's wife, Millie, as a second cash stream aside from her Millie's on Main diner. But they ran into trouble when someone sued them after getting scalded by hot coffee. Yeah, a replay of that charade from the 90s and Mickey Ds. I represented them and we came to a settlement, but the whole thing bled the Mayor and Millie dry. She didn't want to have anything more to do with the business, so I helped them sell by acting as a broker between Big Coffee Shop and the Little Indy Shop. Was happy Millie made out big, letting her pay off the plaintiff and walk away with some spending money.

Annabelle wasn't yet there when I arrived, so I took the liberty of ordering for us, having memorized her drink of choice.

"If it isn't Mr. Junction himself," Cameron said as I walked up to the register, a college kid who worked the espresso machines I knew when he was still in diapers.

"Hey, Cam, how's it hangin'?"

He raised a brow. "Hangin? I'm sorry, but the '90s would like their youthful lingo back."

I frowned and tilted my head, feeling old. "Just take my order, would you?"

He snickers and wiped his hands on his black apron. "What can I get ya, chief?"

"A grande extra-hot flat white with sugar-free vanilla and an extra shot and—"

The kid held up a hand. "Wait, wait, wait. Isn't that Annabelle Kirkland's drink?"

Heat ran up the back of my neck and bloomed in my cheeks. "Uh, yeah," I stammered.

Cameron crossed his arms and grinned, throwing me a knowing wink for good measure. "You two hooking up, or what?"

I frowned. "No, Cam. We're dating, but not—what the hell is it any of your business, anyway? Just make the drink, already!"

The guy cracked up, asking, "Anything else?"

"And a mint tea, if it's not too much to ask."

Another snicker before he finished ringing me up. I paid with my phone then slid down to the end of the bar as he made my drinks.

Snow was really coming down now, Mariah Carey belting "All I Want for Christmas Is You" like she meant it from above. Sort of warmed me up even as the full-length windows all along Main Street sent a chill through me. Cameron finished up the drinks just as the woman of the hour herself arrived.

Grabbing her drink, I met her at the door. Boy, she didn't look good! I mean, she looked *good*. More like she looked *sick*. Now I regretted dragging her along on my date with ulterior motives. Hopefully her drink would cheer her up.

"Hey, babe!" I said, handing Annabelle her fru fru drink as the door slammed behind. "One grande extra-hot flat white with sugar-free vanilla and an extra shot, for the woman of the hour."

Before taking it, she blew a beet-red nose into her tissue. I almost jerked back on instinct, but didn't. Glad I didn't. That would have ruined the mood real quick!

"Sorry," she said, cringing as she stuffed the tissue in her pocket. Now she pouted and gave a little squeal, I think of delight, adding, "And thanks for remembering my favorite order!"

I brightened, offering it back.

Until she put up her hands. "I'm sorry, I can't."

I drew back, my arm sinking some. She must be bad if she turned down her Starbucks drink of choice.

"Mmm, is that a mind tea?" she said through a clouded nose, eyes widening some with delight at the other drink I was holding. My drink.

I held it up, my face falling at what I thought she was getting at. "Uh, yeah."

She smiled at me, those doe eyes of hers fluttering in that way she let them rip when she was going in for the kill.

"Tea sounds real good, babe..." Then she pulled out that tissue again, blowing for good measure.

I handed it over. "It's yours. Gladly."

And she promptly took it, taking a sip and closing her eyes, humming with pleasure. "Just what the doc ordered."

"Good..." I look at her grande extra-hot flat white monstrosity and tried holding my smile.

What men do for love...

"You up for a walk?" I said, taking a sip and sticking out my arm. I winced, but was grateful for the hot drink.

She took another sip of my mint tea and slid it inside. "Gladly."

Landry Jewelers was a few blocks back toward downtown, if you can call the Junction that, so I'd have to play it cool as we walked Main Street. But a quick glance at my watch told me I'd have to hustle it. Only eleven minutes to 1:30 p.m. now. Herb was the punctual type and wouldn't look too kindly on our tardiness.

"Are you going to make it home for Christmas this year?" I started, trying to get her distracted with a question while also curious if she was going to make the trip back to Tennessee.

She took a sip of her tea and shrugged. "Not sure. Things are a bit...shall we say, tense at the moment."

"Tense?"

Annabelle went silent, her hand going to her nose and stifling what I thought was a sniffle, but sounded more like an emerging sob.

I put an arm around her as we walked. "What is it, babe?"

Leaning into me, she shared, "Daddy caught Mama cheatin'."

"What?" I stopped, turning to face her. Eyes were wet and red now.

Another sip before pulling out another tissue and blowing. More from sadness than sickness, surely, but either way I felt bad about what I had planned now. Secretly engagement ring shopping while her family was falling apart...Didn't seem right. Maybe this wasn't such a good idea now.

"What happened, if I can ask?"

"Long story, one I'm really not interested rehashing." She sighed and leaned against me again, wrapping an arm around my waist. "Let's keep walking."

We did, shuffling down icy sidewalks and catching sight of Landry Jewelers a block a head.

Annabelle silently sipped her tea, and I wondered whether we should go through with it.

Just a few doors away. Now or never...

Nearing, I made a quick decision with a swift clearing of my throat.

"Oh, hey, look at that," I said with a chuckle. We stopped, and I pointed at a big fat diamond ring sign hanging above the shop door. "How about we check out Herb's joint?"

She furrowed her brow at me before looking up at the sign. "Landry's Jeweler?"

"Yeah, it'll be fun! Come on—" I opened the door and grabbed her hand before she could object, then whisked her inside.

It was nice and toasty, a welcomed relief from the bitter cold, smelling of new carpet and Lysol and leather. Tiny bright lights shone from tracks in the ceiling down on cases lining the perimeter of the shop at the edge with an island of the same at the center. It was packed, too. Probably a dozen patrons. 'Tis the season for jewelry shopping! Which I suppose made sense, given it was Christmas time.

"This is...nice?" Annabelle said, putting on a brave smile.

"I thought it would be," I replied, heart thumping a mean beat as I searched the room for Herb. He was helping another couple at the back. Looked like John and Jeannie Morgan, with their son Jamal. Smart as a whip, he was. Six going on sixteen.

"What would be?" Annabelle said.

Herb saw me and whispered something to the Morgans. Man was wearing a red and green bow tie at his buttoned collar and a complementary red and green flannel vest over a starch-white shirt with gray slacks. Beady little glasses sat perched on his nose attached to a silver chain that hung with generosity from his neck. Sure knew how to play the part.

I smiled and nodded, and Annabelle pulled at my arm, repeating, "What would be?"

Furrowing my brow, I shook my head. "What?"

"Why are we here?" she whispered in a huffy rush.

Now my face fell. "I thought it would be nice..."

"To look at jewelry while I'm spiking a 100 degree fever?"

"Well...yeah. Like rings and stuff."

Now her jaw dropped and eyes got big. "Rings?" she said in another whispered rush.

Uh, oh...

Maybe this wasn't such a good idea.

But too late now. Herb was approaching with a wide grin. So I made the best of the moment and matched him.

"Gideon O'Donnell," Herb said, extending his hand in a greeting. "Right on time."

Annabelle flashed me another wide-eyed look as I shook his hand, clearly not thrilled and putting the pieces together that I'd arranged it all. This was going to be an interesting hour.

"And Ms. Kirkland," he said, taking her hand now and offering it a peck in that old-school, old-man way. Then he led her and me to the back. "Right this way. It's all arranged."

She glanced back at me with those deer-in-headlights eyes that communicated a mixture of irritation and dread.

Dear Lord, what have I done...

We passed a center island case of watches on toward the back, where a black velvet cloth was draped across a case, bare but for one of those square magnifying glass thingies. Next to it in the corner were the Morgans, glancing up when we arrived with Herb.

Jeannie brightened. "Gideon O'Donnell! Why hello, sir."

I nodded as Herb slipped behind the glass case. "Hi, Mrs. Morgan. John."

The man stuck out a large hand and smiled. "Mr. O'Donnell. Ma'am," John said, nodding to Annabelle, who didn't look thrilled. Not in the slightest.

"What brings you two here?" I asked, trying to distract from Herb's activities.

"Ring shopping, my man!" John answered.

Jeannie frowned and sputtered her lips before gently hitting his arm. "Ring *browsing* is more like it."

"Mama's gonna get a new diamond ring for Christmas!" Jamal said.

To which his Mama promptly smacked him upside the head.

"I ain't neither, boy! Sure is nice, but too rich for our blood."

"Oh, come on, Mama. You deserve it!"

"Listen to the kid, dear," John said. "He's right."

She turned to her husband and frowned even further. "He ain't neither! I don't need no diamond ring for Christmas. I got all the glitz and glamor I need."

John pursed his lips and wrinkled his brow, throwing me a glance that told him he still had some work to do. And I knew he would, too. Could see it in his eyes he was fixing to give his wife the best dang Christmas yet. Whether she liked it or not.

"So why you two here?" Jeannie said, turning to me and Annabelle.

Herb withdrew a large flat box now and started arranging ring bands and diamonds on the black fabric. Big diamonds.

Expensive diamonds.

Jeannie eyed them, eyes widening and jaw dropping. "Is this what I think it is?" A bit too loud for my liking before leaning in with a grin and adding: "Do I see wedding bells in your future?"

I threw Annabelle a glance, feeling the room gawking at us now.

She threw me the same, clearly not thrilled the good folk of Mill Creek were learning some juicy gossip that would surely find its way around the Junction before Christmas! Given our two...shall we say, competing professions—she the local assistant prosecuting attorney, me the resident defense attorney—we'd kept our relationship on the down-low. But now...after Jeannie's announcement—so much for discretion!

"So what're you checking out, pretty lady?" Annabelle asked, leaning toward Jeannie and the glass case they had been standing next to.

"Mama's Christmas gift!" Jamal said excitedly.

She frowned. "I said stop it, boy!"

Then she regarded a ring resting inside a black box still setting on the counter. Nice ring, too. White gold with a very large princess-cut diamond at a center with an intricate weaving of gold surrounding the prongs that served as its setting. Perfect Christmas gift for a lucky lady like Jeannie. Perfect engagement ring for a lucky lady like Annabelle, too.

Annabelle leaned toward it, crossing her arms and *ooing* and *ahhing*. "Get it, girl. If you've got a man willing to toss around some Benjamins for a Christmas gift like this—I say throw caution to the lake effect wind gusting up Main Street and take him up on his offer!"

Jeannie laughed. Problem isn't the tossing around part, but the *possessing* part."

"Baby, I said it's not a problem!" John said, his normally deep, intimidating baritone voice going soft and pleading. "Where there's a will, there's a way!"

"I don't know..." She joined Annabelle looking over the ring and added, "It's an awful lot of money."

"Don't worry, Mama!" Jamal prodded. "It's like Daddy said: Where there's a will, there's a way!"

The two women continued ogling over the ring while Jamal continued pestered his mom to take Dad up on the offer.

As they ogled, John ribbed me and threw me a wink. "Engagement ring shopping ehh, brotha?"

I offered a nervous laugh and went to respond—when I heard the door jangle behind me before slamming shut with enough reverb to rattle the rings.

Then the most god-awful command that set my lizard brain into full-on Jack Bauer mode.

"EVERYBODY FREEZE!"

Everybody did, time itself seeming to obey the command of a gravelly voice that screamed no-nonsense— the sound of the place winding down to a tuning fork ting even as mouths around me opened in fright and surely sent up all kinds of screams and curses and shouts of protest. None of which I heard because that damn fight-or-flight adrenaline kicked into high gear and all senses melded together into one big stew of confusion, along with my heart sending blood galloping through my body in a cold dread and pulsing in my head with activation.

The gunfire immediately snapped me back to the moment.

Once, then twice, a man dropping behind me. Someone I'd seen at Starbucks once or twice, but didn't know his name. Thankfully, not dead or injured, just reacting.

The others joined him, John throwing Jamal to the ground before doing the same to his wife and taking up a position in front to shield them both.

Annabelle was already on her knees by the time I reacted to join John in playing the hero to save my soon-to-be fiancé. Should have guessed she was the last person on the planet who would need saving, but still.

Something from my lizard brain immediately kicked into high gear and it reached for the chivalry that had guided men since the caves. Instead of crouching along with her, I stood in front—feet planted to the carpet, widening some, and hands flexing into fists. Knew they'd do jack squat against that pistol he was carrying, but still. I was ready. For anything.

First thing that hit me in that liminal space between the second gunfire and the ensuing pandemonium was the weapon. 9mm pea-shooter, by the look of it. Pops had taught me well, taking me to the shooting range during summer breaks as a teenager. So I had a pretty good idea what gun was what, and what they could do. Close range, they could do some damage. But from that distance, they were better at scaring the crap out of you than dropping you cold.

But still...the perp was armed. And any armed man was a dangerous man. Especially with what hit me next.

Second thing I noticed was that it was poking out at the end of a bare hand that had seen hard labor, extending up through an arm stuffed inside a battered jean jacket and on toward an even more battered set of overhauls covering a skin-and-bones frame with a chicken head on top—the man's sunken eyes and drooping pale skin and missing teeth and stringy hair telling me all was not right. Sure as heck he was on something—who else but a strung-out druggie would rob a jeweler in broad daylight the week of Christmas?

Regardless, didn't recognize the man in the slightest. Never saw him in Mill Creek, as far as I could remember. Or maybe he was north of the tracks, from the other end of town at the edge of the Junction. But now I would. By God, I would pick the man out of a lineup if and when it came to it. Mark my—

Another *pew-pew-pew* from that peashooter snapped me out from my assessment and to the moment. Accompanying the gunfire was another round of shouts and screams and curses, most of all from Herb Landry.

And in the most unexpected of ways.

"I say, sir, but what the blazes do you think you are doing, barging into my shop?"

I glanced behind to find the man standing tall in front of the black velvet cloth he had draped across the back case for our meeting. Looking as spry and dapper as ever, with that bowtie pulled tight and his vest smoothed of any wrinkles, chest puffed out and head held high.

But...

What the heck was the man thinking?

"Herb," Annabelle whispered, "back down!"

Landry didn't respond. Just stood there, tall and unyielding.

Instead, he said to the perp, "The police will be on their way shortly, as I've engaged a security measure for such times. So I suggest you leave the way you came."

The revelation sent a jittering jolt through the man, that sleeve of the battered jean jacket waving like a storm-battered sail—and the peashooter taking aim along with it!

But he didn't shoot. And he didn't leave the way he came.

Instead, the assailant stepped farther into the store, to the watch case. "I've only come for the watch. Then I'll be on my way. No one gets hurt. Nothin' gets stolen. No harm no foul."

He twitched funny. A sort of head jerk with an added right brow raise. Then he scratched at his forearm. The one holding the peashooter. All absentminded and autopilot, like it was part of his minute-by-minute existence.

I frowned, knowing I'd called that one. Telltale signs of a junkie. Opioids, maybe. Lord knows the Junction had been dealt its own bad hand of that slice of the national crisis.

"The watch?" Herb said, eyes squinting and head tilting with inquiry.

"*YOU KNOW THE WATCH!!*" the man yelled at the top of his lungs, face going cranberry red and carotid artery bulging with rage.

Which sent up another flair of screams and shouts and curses almost worse than when the peashooter fired. And it made perfect sense, too. Because a raging man is more dangerous than a peashooter any day of the week.

Now Herb himself startled, and his face also seemed to register something now, finally.

Recognition.

"And if you don't hop to it," the assailant said, more measured now and reaching the center island of gleaming cases, "I'm gonna drop you right now and take it all. Because that watch belonged to my dad, and granddad before him. Daddy's dyin' of d'mencha, but the only thing he remembers is that watch. Given to him one Christmas when he turned thirteen. Keeps goin' on and on 'bout it..."

Another twitching head jerk, more scratching at the arm, the man mumbling under is breath and shuffling farther in.

To which Herb responded by meeting him step for step. "Now, see here. I paid you fare and square!"

"For god's sake, Herb," I muttered, sighing and dipping my head with anger. "Hand it over, already!"

Herb glanced behind, hissing, "Stay out of this, Gideon. I dealt with this ruffian once. I can deal with him—"

Suddenly, the case behind us shattered with the deafening crash of glass, shards of it scattering across the surrounding carpet like diamonds.

Which some probably were, since it was the case we'd been standing at before things went sour.

So much for engagement ring shopping!

"Next time it's your head," the man said calmly before adding: "*NOW HAND IT OVER!!!*"

Herb hopped to it now. No questions asked. He beelined it for the center cases, fumbling with his keys along the way and muttering to himself.

The junkie aimed straight for his head the whole time. But none of that nervous twitching now, thank god. I'd worried the man might slip scratching at himself again.

Didn't take long before Herb pulled out a thick watch case and opened it for inspection. Inching forward, the junkie trained the 9mm at the man's head and craned toward gold watch glistening under all those lights.

A twitching smile struggled for a hearing across his face, whether from the drugs or delight, wasn't sure. But soon it was over.

Without saying a word, or firing his gun again, the junkie rushed for the exit, threw open the door with a thud, then dashed away with his watch—and our dignity after being violated so. The whole thing made me regret the times I've represented such scumbags in court.

Sirens were wailing now in the distance through the open door. As always, impeccable timing by Mill Creek Junction's finest.

Frowning and shaking my head, I went to my knees and spun around, throwing my arms around Annabelle. Her nose was read and eyes puffy, but both were probably from her cold. Other than that, she was fine.

Thank God she was fine!

"You alright, Gideon?" she asked first.

A sudden shake took hold of my body, and my bowels went all watery, the adrenaline from it all settling down and leaving behind the realization of what had happened. Not only the robbery, but how close we'd all come to getting clocked by the junkie lunatic, if it came to that.

But I nodded, squeezing her tighter. "I'm fine. You?" I asked, pulling back and holding Annabelle at her shoulders. Taking in her beautiful face and thanking God for real she was fine, searching her eyes for fright but finding none. Which wasn't a surprise. Far tougher than I was!

She flashed me a smile and nodded, burrowing into my chest. We held each other, saying nothing more, John and

Jeannie and Jamal doing the same behind us but with far more excited utterances.

Soon, three uniformed officers barreled into the shop, carried along by a bout of cold winter wind gusting through the open door. Chief Roller was close behind, along with a few EMTs, their reds-and-blues, reds-and-whites flashing now outside. They checked on us and started taking statements. Annabelle and I went to the chief ourselves and explained what happened. Her more than I, given her official capacity with the city.

Finishing with the chief, I went to check on Herb when he came up to me instead.

"Gideon," he whispered in my ear. "A word, please..."

He grabbed my arm, and before I could ask what was up, he gently pulled me back and nodded toward the cases where we'd been set to look at rings.

I caught Annabelle's attention as we headed back, shrugging as she cocked her head with inquiry. She followed close behind, looking as confused as I was.

We went back to the cases where we'd been before the afternoon went to hell. The box of diamonds and ring settings Herb had pulled for us was toppled on the floor, its contents strewn about and mingled with the shattered glass. I could see empty white-gold settings glistening from the carpet, but the diamonds were another story.

Leaning in, Herb whispered in a rush, "It's missing!"

"What's missing?" I said, glancing down at the glass crunching under my shifting weight.

"No. Not those..." He guided me to the other case, where the Morgans had been. "This one."

He pointed to the top and folded his arms, pressing his lips into a thin line and regarding me with knowing eyes.

Didn't get his drift at first.

And then I did.

The ring Jeannie and Annabelle had been ogling over right before the junkie burst into the shop! The one John and Jamal had wanted his mom to get, but Jeannie insisted they couldn't afford.

I wasn't at all liking what Herb was implying.

This day just went from bad to crap in a hot second...

"Now, now," I said, putting up both hands like I did in the courtroom. "We can't jump to conclusions, Herb!"

"But you saw it!" he retorted, stomping his foot for good measure. "Both of you."

"I don't understand," Annabelle said. "What are you getting at?"

Herb gestured wildly at the case now, his own carotid artery bulging with indignation. "The ring, right there in its case. Did you and Jeannie remove it, Annabelle?"

Furrowing her brow, she folded her arms and shook her head. "No, we didn't..."

Herb clapped his hands together. "That's it then!"

She threw me a glance I'd seen before when she was uncomfortable. "What's it then?"

"Jeannie stole the ring!"

"Oh, come on, Herb!" I said.

"Or John, I suppose..."

"No way. No how!"

Herb pivoted to Annabelle now, eyes and arms wide with plea. "You have a duty, Ms. Kirkland, as a law enforcement officer to track down that diamond ring!"

Annabelle stepped back and put up a hand of her own. "First of all, I'm not law enforcement. I'm a prosecutor. This isn't my line of work."

"But she *stole* it, for Pete's sake!"

Herb was getting animated, and the blues were looking over. Even the chief looked like he was about to intervene.

"Second of all…" Annabelle said, not letting the man take over, "we don't know jack crap! Who knows what happened to it. Could have tumbled to the ground in all the confusion."

"Didn't. I checked."

"Alright, then. Maybe someone else took it during the confusion."

"Did you see anyone come our way?"

He was looking at me now. I brought a hand to my chin, feeling super uncomfortable with the interrogation. But…I had to hand it to the guy. He was right. No one else had bothered coming our way. Everyone pretty much stuck to their huddled position until interviewed by MCPD. So the idea that the ring had been swiped by someone else…

But the Morgans? No way! And something in the back of my lizard brain began flaring up all kinds of things that suggested the man was fingering them because they were the only non-white patrons of his establishment that day. Could be that I was sensitive to racial profiling since my own adoptive father had been fingered more than I'd care to imagine; being a white boy of black adoptive parents opened my eyes to things I wished I had only read about in history books.

Then again, the man made some sense. And if he was about to finger the Morgans, rightly or wrongly, the least I could do was try to intervene, given my history as their attorney.

I put a gentle hand on his arm and suggested, "Let me go talk to them. See if I can straighten this out. I've represented them before on other matters—not at all criminal," I felt I needed to add.

He regarded me through those beady little glasses perched on his nose. "I don't know…"

"As an officer of the court," Annabelle said, "I support that idea. In fact, we'll both go." She smiled at me and nodded, her eyes telling me to take the deal.

It was a good deal, so I did.

"We'll head over right now and sort this out. In the meantime—no MCPD, no Chief Roller, alright?"

Herb glanced over my shoulder to the chief himself, conferring with a detective. The man seemed to perk up and look our way, as if sensing we were talking about him.

But the jeweler nodded with a sigh. "I'll give you an hour or two to sort this out." He held up a finger and added with a whisper, "But then I'm going to Chief Roller himself!"

I nodded. "Fine. We'll be back—two hours, tops."

He held up two fingers, then sauntered away.

No time like the present to get to the bottom of a day that went to hell on skis.

"So much for a nice relaxing afternoon on the town…" I muttered as we hustled for the door.

"Always an adventure with you, Gideon," she said before blowing her nose. "Always an adventure."

I smiled and nodded at the chief as we passed, then pushed through the exit. "Next time, pizza and Netflix. Promise."

"I'm holding you to that."

Since I had walked from my house, we took Annabelle's BMW. Wasn't an Audi, but it did the job.

"Come on, Gideon, level with me," she said, heading down Main Street for the fifteen minute drive to the Morgans, the sun dipping below the horizon now and sending long shadows across the main drag. "Does this ring true?"

I threw her a frown. "Are you asking as my girlfriend who cares about the Morgans' interests, or as the Mill Creek assistant prosecutor?"

And she threw me a look that said just answer the damn question. Understood it was both, given the grand theft nature of it all.

I took a breath, propping my elbow on my window and shaking my head. "Doesn't make sense in the slightest. This isn't like them at all."

"Never been in trouble with the law?"

"Not if you count Jamal going missing this past summer and sending the MCPD on a wild goose chase all day because his friend needed a pair of shoes!"

"Alright, calm down," she corrected, turning down the Morgan's street now, a sad part of town at the edge of Mill Creek that was close to the leftover railroad tracks that had put the Junction on the map.

"Sorry. I'm just still on edge from everything."

She reached over and grabbed my hand, squeezing it three times.

I. Love. You.

I smiled, feeling warmer now at her touch. Our secret signal.

Looking at her, I squeezed it one-two-three times before adding a final shaking squeeze.

I. Love. You. Toooo!

We arrived at a shotgun-style house covered with snow, the sun having receded completely now to darkness. Last time I was here was when Jamal went missing, and I remember reading somewhere in some bargain-bin Kindle mystery novel about why the types of houses were named as such: front door went straight to the back door, with rooms off the main hallway you could pop off a shot straight through without hitting a thing. Only in their case, it would sail through to the garage, but still. Interesting house, and interesting circumstances that brought me back.

Annabelle parked, and I got out. "Let me do the talking, alright? Can't imagine they'll be too thrilled saying anything with the local assistant prosecuting attorney present."

She grabbed my arm before I could get out. "I'm here as your girlfriend this time, alright?"

I smiled and nodded, then headed to the front door.

Nearly slipped on the unshoveled walkway, but managed to keep it together.

I hesitated before rapping against the chipped, faded forest-green door. Felt like the biggest tool, coming up here the week of Christmas to accuse them of stealing a ring. But then I knew it would be worse if Herb went full Herb Landry and got the chief involved.

So rap I went. Three times, then two more.

Didn't take long before Jeannie was at the door, face looking like she'd run a marathon—I could empathize, the afternoon's events catching up with me now too. Wanted nothing more than to take a hot shower and nurse a bottle of scotch. But I got to it.

"Hey, Jeannie, sorry to bother you—"

"Everything alright? We already talked to the police." She was glancing at Annabelle now, addressing her statement to her.

"It's not about that," I went on. "Well, it sort of is—can we come in?"

I gestured inside the warm home smelling of leftover lasagna, and she obliged. John was coming toward us now, beer in one hand. Jamal wasn't anywhere, which made sense. I would have put my kid to bed as soon as I got home too, after what happened.

"What's this about?" John asked.

I looked to Annabelle, who nodded me onward. I told them why we were there. And everything Herb had said.

"That man thinks *we* stole it?" John exploded, throwing back a swig of beer before slamming it on the counter.

"I completely understand," I said.

"No, Gideon," Jeannie said. "I don't think you do!"

I took a breath and glanced at Annabelle, seeking back up now. From the Junction APA as much as my girlfriend!

And she delivered.

"Look, Mrs. Morgan, we're not looking to make trouble. And we're not looking to make this...legal. We just want to head off anything before it becomes a thing. Do you understand?"

Jeannie crossed her arms and leaned against the countertop, saying nothing.

"Do you know anything?" I said. "Anything at all. Perhaps the ring fell somewhere during the robbery. Or—"

Jeannie gasped, putting a hand to her mouth before muttering something to herself. Then she stood stiffly and sauntered down the shotgun hallway without saying a word.

John looked at us and motioned for us to follow. "You heard the woman. Sounds like she's got your answer."

She was already at Jamal's bed when we arrived, light on and poor kid's ear at the end of her pinched fingers.

"Tell 'em!" she bellowed.

"Oww, Mama!" Jamal shouted with pain.

"Boy, if you don't fess up now—"

"Alright! I swiped it!"

John sucked in a breath. Thought he'd grab his other ear, but he said instead, "You stole the ring?"

Poor kid's lower lip started quivering. Right before his eyes welled up with tears and he clenched them tight, his body starting to shake and a wail that sounded like 'Sorry, Mama!' erupting from him. Broke my heart. And Jeannie's.

She scooped him up and held him close, Jamal's glasses smushing against her as his head burrowed against her shoulder, Jeannie doing what a good mother does: reassuring her scared son it'll be alright.

Went on like this for another minute or two until she brought him out for a good talking to.

Holding the kid by the shoulders, she looked him square in the face. "Time to calm yourself and fess up. What's this about you goin' on swipin' from poor ol' Herb Landry?"

Wiping his eyes, Jamal said, "I just wanted you to have a nice present. One fit for a Queen Mama! You don't ever do nothin' nice for yourself, and I just thought you should have it."

Then he buried his head back in Jeannie's chest and started crying again.

Jeannie and John said nothing. I glanced around the room and spotted a small black box on the kid's dresser. Walking over, I chuckled to myself. Didn't even try to hide it. Not yet, anyway.

I picked it up and opened the top. Nice ring. Perfect, really...

Then I stuffed it in my coat pocket and said softly, "I'll take care of it."

"Thank you," Jeannie mouthed back, still holding her son crying as much from getting caught stealing as from the crazy afternoon, I imagined.

I went to leave when John grabbed my arm. He held out his hand and said, "Thanks, Gideon. We owe you."

I took and smiled. "No, you don't. Merry Christmas,

John."

Then we left and headed back to Landry Jewelers.

It was a short ride back into town. We didn't say much, the day settling in hard now as evening waned into night.

Annabelle drove us back, and I gazed outside in thought, my hand inside my pocket rocking the black ring case back and forth. It was all too much for a humble defense attorney who meant to practice corporate litigation but wound up back home in small-town USA. Sure made me think about life's big questions.

Which made me do the other thing I hadn't planned on, but figured was as good a time as any.

Near-death experiences with jewelry store robbery makes you do a thing like that.

"Pull over," I said, gesturing to the parking lot of First Bank of Mill Creek.

"What, why?" Annabelle asked.

"Just do it, alright? Got something to say."

She went to object but instead muttered something to herself about knowing better, whatever that meant.

She slid next to a handicap spot and barely put her BMW into park when I let the question slip: "Annabelle Kirkland, will you marry me?"

Annabelle threw up a startled squeal, and looked my way as I was holding up the little black case, open. The moonlight caught the ring just right, with snow gently falling on the windshield.

She didn't say anything. Only sat there with her hands at her mouth. So I did.

"Wasn't planning to do this now, but after all that had happened, it reminded me how fleeting life is. How things can turn on a dime. One minute you're shopping for rings. The next you're in the middle of an armed robbery and defending a kid against theft. Sort of puts things into perspective."

Another squeal, hand still at her mouth. At least she was nodding now.

"And with all that's wrong in the world, I know we can put it right. Together. Bit by bit. There's no one I'd rather spend the rest of my life with so...will you?"

Didn't take her long until she was sobbing with arms around my neck.

"Yes, Gideon O'Donnell. Yes, yes, *yes!*"

We cried and laughed, then cheered us.

Finally, I pulled away and smiled. "Let's go get Herb his ring back. Well, our ring—right after we pay for it!"

And we did, trotting back to Landry's Jeweler the few blocks from the bank with the euphoria of engagement to carry us through another bout of lake effect snow pummeling Main Street. The big chunky kind that cakes your hair and fills your nostrils. But we didn't care. Along the way, we opened our mouth and let it in, giggling like high schoolers.

Can't say Herb was too pleased with Jamal's theft. He understood it and all, how and why it went down, and I assured him he'd be more than set on the straight-and-narrow by his mom and dad, so that seemed to suffice. It probably helped that I bought the ring with a nice, fat check.

I was just thankful he promised not to prosecute on top of Annabelle saying yes! So Jamal and his family were safe, and I was set to marry the most beautiful woman on the planet.

Two good deeds for the price of one.

Can't get any better way to ring in the season than that the week of Christmas!

The Reason for the Season

If Peter Daniel Young was known for one thing and one thing alone, it's that he gets the job done, no matter what.

He's a doer. A go-getter. The guy you call when you want a job done the right way the first time.

Except when there's a Mill Creek Junction Christmas pageant to have to plan, apparently!

Almost two weeks until Christmas Eve and I still had all the major outstanding parts to fill.

Needed another shepherd, not to mention the sheep and cattle that were usually the staple of Mill Creek Junction's production. The Three Wise Men were still waiting to be filled. Still had no angels. Which was an odd problem since all they had to do was just stand there in white robes and spout off one line: *"'Glory to God in the highest heaven, and on earth peace to those on whom his favor rests.'"* Not hard when you're in a group.

Then there was the more worrisome of the bunch: Mary and Joseph and baby Jesus!

You might be able to get away with a Christmas pageant

without the Three Wise Men, since they didn't really come into play until Jesus was older. Maybe the shepherds; definitely without the live sheep and cattle. But the main attraction? No Mary, no Joseph, no Baby Jesus? And with practice tomorrow?

Yeah, I was screwed.

What the heck was I thinking waiting so long?

I buried my head in my hands as I sat in my church office. I'd exhausted every avenue at Mill Creek Baptist I was told to exhaust. Reverend Alden, the former minister, had given me a list of names before he headed down to Florida for the winter. Snow birds, they call them. What I wouldn't like to be sitting on a beach right now...

Unfortunately, most of the list was either out of town that day or not feeling the vibe.

Which meant I was screwed. How I was ever going to fill all the pageant roles in time would take a true Christmas miracle.

Lord, throw me a bone here!

There was a soft knock at the door.

I dropped my hands and raised my hands. "Come in."

The door opened. It was Katrina, my sweet-mannered administrative assistant. Reminded me more of my grandma than anyone who should be assisting me. Not that I didn't need it; administration certainly wasn't my spiritual gift. I'd just felt weird when I started pastoring at Mill Creek bossing someone around who looked like the woman who slapped me around and set me straight my whole life. Wasn't fond of giving orders, but Katrina was more than willing to help out and put me on a good administrative footing. Even slapping me around a bit!

"Hey, Kat," I said, the name I liked to call her. Usually

made her giggle, because it made her sound forty years younger than she was.

Katrina giggled just then, her silver curls bouncing at her shoulders and her glasses sliding down her face. She frowned and put her hands on her hips. "Why so glum, Reverend? You look like death rolled over you."

I almost corrected her, telling her Peter was just fine. Never could get used to the whole Reverend moniker. But I didn't. Knew that's what she knew, and that was fine.

Instead, I sighed and leaned back in my chair, playing with a pen. "It's just this darn Christmas pageant."

She took a step inside now, her hands falling to her side. "What do you mean? What's wrong with the pageant?"

I tossed the pen to the desk. "I can't get anyone to commit, that's what's wrong! I've got a few teenage shepherds, but no angels. That's not even touching on the fact I've got no main attraction."

Katrina gasped. "Don't tell me you don't have the baby Jesus part..."

I sighed again, heavier than I intended. I sat forward to my desk and brought my hands to my face. Rubbing it, I answered, "Not only that, but his ma and pa are MIA as well."

"No!"

I nodded. "Same for the Three Wise Men."

She batted at me dismissively. "Yeah, but everyone knows they didn't show up until Jesus was older."

"Tell that to the people who wrote the dang Christmas pageant!"

"So what are you going to do?"

I shrugged. "What can I do? I've got no one left in Mill Creek Baptist. No one who would be able or capable of pageanting."

Katrina chuckled. "Nice gerund there, sonny. Why don't you go out and shake some bushes?"

I leaned back again in my chair, curious. "What do you mean, shake some bushes?"

She spread her arms out toward the door. "You've got a whole small town who'd be more than interested in helping you out."

I followed her gesturing. "Really? Like, just go ask Junction folk if they want to sign up to play the parts?"

"Well, you'd have to be strategic about it, know who you're picking and why. And more importantly, who not to pick and why."

"And how the heck am I going to know that?"

"Why, the Holy Spirit, darlin'!" Then she gave me a wink and shuffled off to make photocopies.

This whole pastoring gig was more than I bargained for.

Before I left, Katrina snagged me and gave me a few suggestions, apparently channeling the Holy Spirit's guidance and direction. Then she sent me off with a Starbucks gift card and a promise of prayer.

And off I went, trudging down the Mill Creek Baptist driveway and on to Main Street, snow piled high on either side of the sidewalk. At least it was cleared, mostly, some of the less-than mindful households doing a half-baked job at doing their part at maintaining a pathway for folks walking into and from town. There was a bite to the air, too. At least it wasn't moving, and there were traces of spice and woodsmoke floating through it, which helped. The sun did too, its round, bright orb high in a clear mid-morning sky, reflecting off the powder-white snow layered on the trees and piled like cakes on front yards with a special brilliance that day. Seemed like a good sign of the Spirit, the way the day felt walking into town.

Gave me enough confidence to shake some bushes, as Kat suggested.

But first things first: putting that gift card to good use. A grande gingerbread latte had my name on it.

Strolling up to the corporate behemoth that had commodified the connoisseurial coffee experience, I had a ping of regret knowing how the little guys like my girlfriend struggled to compete with the suburban staple. But there wasn't nothing else in Mill Creek, and I needed my favorite festive holiday drink to get me through the day. So I yanked open the door, the warm air heavy with roasted coffee beans and sugary baked goods slapping me in the face, and I prayed to the good Lord above Lexi didn't find out. Because boy, would she make me pay!

Not a bad looking joint. A quaint thing of exposed wood and brick that was several stories above the run-of-the-mill strip mall varieties. Sort of bespoke its Midwest roots stretching back to the founding of the Junction in the 1800s. I learned it used to be one of the little guys back in the day, a little bitty coffee shop owned by Mayor Goodall's wife, Millie, as a second cash stream aside from her diner. Not sure what happened, but they had to close that down and consolidate to their one restaurant. Glad they kept that, because Millie's breakfast was to die for! But that opened a door for the dreaded Siren to come and swing its 400-pound weight around to capitalize on the coffee traffic. Another piece of small-town America lost its soul along the way, and I'm sure a pixie somewhere keeled over as well.

I'm a sucker for Starbucks like most—don't tell Lexi— but sometimes Corporate America really sucks. Although the exposed wood and brick wasn't bad. Made it that the more tolerable.

The place was half full and there was no line. I strolled

to the counter and gave a nod to Cameron, my favorite small-town barista.

"How ya doing, pastorman?" he said, the college kid manning the espresso machine with gauges the size of nickels, a crown of blond hair stuffed under a navy stocking cap. He sort of had that boy-next-door look about him, but was trying to pull a bad-boy look that looked like fake news. He wasn't fooling anyone.

"Pretty good, Cameron, pretty good. You finish that book I lent you?"

"For sure! That Lewis guy is pretty tight."

I raised a brow. Tight? Kids these days.

I'd lent the guy my copy of C. S. Lewis's *Mere Christianity*. Had gotten me through some tough times of doubt when everything was up in the air regarding my faith a few years ago. Sort of began reimagining the faith, and then when I'd discovered a cancerous tumor, it all fell apart. Almost walked away had it not been for his guidance. Thought Cameron could use it to help him navigate his own spiritual journey.

"So, what did you think?" I asked. "Especially his argument about Jesus being a liar, lunatic, or Lord?"

He left the espresso machine and sidled up to the register, getting animated now. "See, I had this idea that there could be another 'L' word."

The junior up at the Mill Creek Community College leaned in like he was about to drop a knowledge bomb on the Junction's newest pastorman.

He leaned forward and whispered, "Legend," then smiled.

I loved it when people were eager to best me. Showed they were using their brains and trying. But that argument wasn't new. Pop theologians and genre novelists with a

Christian ax to grind had recycled it from dead Germans for years.

But I played along. "Interesting," I said. "Go on."

Cameron's eyes widened slightly with delight now. "The way I see it, maybe Jesus' disciples had created all of these stories to sort of keep his memory alive after he died. You know, like the Roman hero narratives. Jesus' disciples made him legendary."

I nodded and brought my eyebrows together as if I were contemplating Cameron's fresh insight.

He crossed his arms in satisfaction. "So, what do you think?"

"I think I like your thinking." I slapped his shoulder and added, "Let's talk sometime, maybe grab coffee or something." Then I looked around at the joint and chuckled. "Or maybe a drink at Max's Place."

"For sure! I'd be down."

"Nice. Well, speaking of which, I'd like a grande gingerbread latte, extra hot."

"Sorry, bro, but we're all out of gingerbread syrup."

"What? No!"

"Bummer, I know. And wouldn't you know, we literally just ran out before you walked through the door. Isn't that ironic?"

I hummed a weak agreement. Just my luck, them being out of my go-to holiday drink. Not a good start to my pageant mission.

"Anything else I can get you?" he asked, moving it along.

I glanced at the menu, wondering what my coffee-shop owner girlfriend would get. Strike that. She'd probably kill me if she knew I was patronizing Starbucks! Or is it patronageing? Is that even a word?

There was a subtle but distinct clearing of the throat.

I chuckled. "Sorry. How about a peppermint and vanilla latte? Those syrups still in stock?"

"Sure thing," he said, writing it up on the side of my Christmas-red cup. "Have it right up for ya."

I thanked Cameron and slid to the end of the bar to wait for my second-best drink. When the door jangled and in walked Gideon O'Donnell and Annabelle Kirkland.

Just the pair I wanted to talk with!

Leaning against the bar, I brought a hand to my chin to assess the situation, like a lion stalking its prey.

They didn't see me. Didn't really look into the place, instead bolting to an open table by the window, the pair both offering furtive, wide gestures. Looked like they were in a heated conversation. Couldn't tell what about with the espresso bean grinder whirling away behind my head on top of the din of conversation, but I wondered if it would spoil my going in for the kill.

A minute later, Cameron announced my drink, setting it on the bar behind me.

"Thanks, man," I said, grabbing it and taking a sip. I hummed, the extra-hot minty vanilla concoction laced with the smokey caramel of roasted espresso beans just what I needed.

I went to leave when I had a thought. "Hey, you wouldn't be interested in playing a part in my Christmas pageant, would you?"

Returning to the espresso machine, Cameron raised a brow. "A Christmas pageant?"

I went to explain but left it alone. "You know what, don't worry about it. Thanks, and let's get a drink to talk over that Lewis book soon, alright?"

He agreed, and I wandered over to Gideon and

Annabelle, taking a long pull of my latte again, then another for good measure.

I was going to need it.

"No way you get past discovery," I heard from Gideon above the din of Starbucks noise.

"And I swear, Gideon, if you ask for one more continuance," I heard from Annabelle on approach, "I'm gonna rip your eyes out and feed them to—"

"Pastor Young..." Gideon said, throwing on a grin and standing.

Annabelle startled and slowly turned, face falling with mortification before rising with an embarrassed grin.

"Hey, Gideon!" I said, holding my drink while reaching out with my other hand. "And it's Peter. Pastor was for Alden, my senior colleague before he left."

He took it. "Right, my bad."

"Uh, hi there, Peter," Annabelle said, offering me her hand as well from her chair.

I took it. "How are you two? Looked like you were in the middle of a heated discussion, so sorry to impose."

They laughed.

Gideon said, "No, just friendly banter—"

"Between two professional," Annabelle added.

"Zero heat." Gideon sat, and the two glanced at each other, their faces both reddening.

Alright then. No need to beat around the bush, so I cleared my throat and went for it. "Say, I was meaning to connect with you both, so it's providential you both walked in while I was grabbing coffee!"

Annabelle glanced at Gideon, a deer-in-headlights look suddenly coming to her eyes.

"Nothing bad or anything," I said with a chuckle. "But

the thing is, I've been tasked with organizing the Mill Creek Junction Christmas pageant this year."

Gideon snorted a laugh. "Oh, yeah, I heard Mayor Goodall roped you into that one this year. Sorry, bro."

"So, here's the thing," I said, pushing on and getting to business. "I was hoping you two would play Mary and Joseph."

The pair went silent. Then at once they looked at me, sat up straight, and started laughing.

From the gut, out the nose and mouth, even from their ears, it seemed.

I smiled and added a chuckle myself, looking around as we started attracting stares.

"Me, Joseph?" Gideon managed, glancing at me before returning to Annabelle. And promptly laughing again.

Annabelle couldn't even reply, she was giggling so hard.

"So...is that a yes?" I said, sure it wasn't but pushing for an answer anyway.

The pair finally composed themselves. Gideon said, "I don't know, Pete. I haven't been to that church for years."

"Doesn't matter. You'd be great. Plus, don't your parents still attend?"

"Yes, but—"

"Then I'm sure they'd love to see their son playing the part of Joseph!"

Not letting Gideon get a word in edge-wise, I turned to Annabelle. "And you're in, Annabelle? Because I seem to remember you visiting once."

Her face got serious all of a sudden. "Yes, that is true."

"So you've got a church background then, right?"

"Yes, I do but—"

"And I'm sure you understand a Christmas pageant can't happen without a Mary, right?"

"Yes, I do, but—"

"And you wouldn't want to make Mayor Goodall disappointed, would you, if we can't find a Mary, right?"

"No, I wouldn't, but—"

"Then it's settled?" I said, nodding her to acceptance.

Annabelle took a breath, ready to say more, but she closed her mouth and tilted her head. Whether considering what I said or disbelieving I was actually talking her into it, I couldn't tell.

A few beats passed before she looked at Gideon, who shrugged. She frowned and said, "Alright, mister. Not sure how you managed to rope us is, but sounds like you've got yourself a superpower I don't know about."

"And it means I've got a Mary at least?"

"Sure, I'm in."

Yes! I said silently to myself.

"Thanks, Annabelle. I owe you!"

She pointed at me, one end of her mouth curling upward. "Yeah, you do. Big time."

"That's great, but..." I said, my face falling. "I'm still short a Joseph. And with the kind of chemistry you two have..."

She snapped her head toward Gideon. "Chemistry?"

"Yeah. I mean, with how you work together on cases."

"*Against* each other," Gideon corrected.

"Even better! You've clearly got to tango to see that justice is served, right? So I just figured, if you've got that kind of dynamic in the courtroom, then surely you would shine on stage. Especially since there really aren't any lines to memorize or anything, and all you have to do is look the part and—"

"Alright, Peter," Gideon said, putting up a hand. "You've roped me in too."

"Really?"

"Had me at my parents, actually, being proud of their son playing Joseph and all that jazz."

I raised my cup in a mock cheer and took a swig of pepperminty vanilla, the smokey caramel espresso more bitter now that the milk had cooled. But it didn't matter. I'd succeeded.

"Thanks, you two. I'll send you the details about practice and then the main event. Which is tomorrow, by the way. Not the main event, but practice."

"*Tomorrow?*" the pair said together.

"9 a.m. sharp. See you then!" I left before they could protest.

Draining my drink, I tossed the cup in the trash can before stepping back out on Main Street. All that negotiating made me hungry! Time for lunch. Which meant time for Millie's on Main. She had a mean burger, and after that conversation I was a man in need.

The sun was high now at the stroke of noon. I was rapidly losing time, and I sort of felt bad for taking a break with all those bushes to shake, as Katrina had suggested. But I was famished! And Peter Daniel Young was no fun when he was famished. So off I strolled down Main Street, picking up my pace toward Millie's on Main and fantasizing about that burger now.

The town reminded me a lot of Coopersville, the small town west of Grand Rapids where I'd grown up and then boomeranged back to after everything got messed up in Washington, DC.

Like the Junction, Coopersville's Main Street bore witness to a simpler era, when neighbors whiled away the morning hours over grits and coffee; when family farmers raked in a sizable wage from an honest week's work; when church and faith sat squarely at the center of the small town's orbit. While small diners still existed, they struggled. While farmers still farmed, they existed as consolidated corporate conglomerates. While churches still existed, they did so at the periphery. While Coopersville still existed, it did so as an also-ran, quaint cliché.

Suppose the same could be said of Mill Creek Junction, and most other small towns.

Strolling up to Millie's, a bell above the door jangled as I entered. The place smelled like frying beef and cheese and potatoes. Perhaps it was because I had a hankering for a burger, so it was all psychological, but this was on top of the smell of pies and cookies and slices of carrot cake that stood proudly displayed at the front counter. Either way, I was sold!

Now for a table...

Searching for one, I spotted someone in the back that gave me an idea.

There was Johnny Pope in his spot in the back corner, nursing a cup of coffee and a plate of what looked like eggs and bacon with toast. He was deep in a newspaper, and I felt bad disturbing him, but...

Yeah, he was exactly who I needed!

So, bypassing the hostess, who was a bit frazzled pulling double-duty waiting on folks seated at the bar anyway, I wandered toward the back, gearing myself up for my ask.

"A little late for breakfast, isn't it?" I said, strolling up to Johnny's table.

Johnny looked up from his paper and folded it, answering gruffly, "It's never too late for breakfast."

I chuckled. "Good answer, and good man. Three meals a day, that's what I say about breakfast."

He smiled. "Amen to that. What brings you by, Rev?"

"Rev? No, no. Peter's fine."

"No, I like Rev. You're not The Rev, like Alden. Just his successor. Or would you prefer Max Blade's preacherman?"

Now I laughed. "Uh, probably not. But either seems too stuffy to me. Peter's fine."

Johnny smirked and unfolded his newspaper, unfurling it and getting back to it. "Try Father on for size. That took me a while to get used to. Sorry, kid. Part of the gig, the honorifics and all."

"Sure, I guess so."

The same awkward silence settled as at Starbucks with Gideon and Annabelle. I really wasn't very good at this sort of thing, asking for people to help and all. Sort of a new thing for me, much more preferring to go it alone. Not because I thought I was better than others or could do it better. Hated bothering people and inconveniencing them.

"You're still here, Rev," Johnny said, head still in his newspaper. "Something I can do you for?"

I coughed and cleared my throat. Here we go.

"Yeah, there is, actually. Sort of providential to see you here."

"Really? How?"

I opened my mouth, but words didn't come. "Never mind. But seeing you here made me think of something."

"Spit it out, kid. My eggs are getting cold." He stabbed a forkful and shoved them in his mouth, still reading his newspaper and giving me the willies at the way he stabbed those eggs. Guy could do some serious damage with a fork!

I took a breath and shifted, folding my arms. "Alright, here's the deal. I've been tasked with putting on this year's Mill Creek Christmas pageant."

Johnny snorted a laugh. "Yeah, I heard Mayor Goodall roped you into that."

I frowned. "That's what Gideon said."

"That's because he knows better."

"Anyway, I chose to do the Christmas story, from Luke's Gospel."

"Sounds about right, you being a reverend and all."

"And I'd like for you to be the narrator," I said, just going for it.

Johnny's eyes appeared above the paper now.

"Excuse me?"

I cleared my throat. "That's right. The script calls for a narrator to sort of read the original Lukan narrative while everyone else acts it out, and I thought you'd be perfect. So, what do you say?"

"At your Protestant Baptist church?"

"Well, it's for the town's Christmas pageant, but yeah."

"But I'm a former Catholic priest."

"Even better!"

Johnny set down his paper and rubbed his chin, looking outside.

"Look, all you have to do is read—" I fished out a folded spiral-bound book from the inside of my coat. Then I pointed out the lines. "It's just these lines."

He squinted and leaned in, then he looked at me and frowned. "That's like the whole thing."

I took a look myself, scanning through the script. He was right. "Look, I'm desperate, alright?"

He leaned back and folded his arms. "Desperate?"

"Uh, no. I didn't mean it like that. It's just, I need a narrator. And I like your voice."

His brow furrowed. "You like my voice?"

This wasn't going well.

"Yeah, you've got the whole James Earl Jones thing going on."

"You're saying I sound like Vader?"

I cocked my head. "No, I'm thinking more like Mufasa than Vader."

Johnny smirked. "That's a relief."

"Come on, man! Do me a solid, will you?"

"A solid? Haven't heard that since the decade before you were born!"

"When do you think I was born?"

"Oh, come on. You're as young as the day is long. 1980, '81 at the latest."

I frowned. "Yeah, well, anyway...I'm in a bind. And I'm told you're the guy to go to when you're in a bind. And being a former priest and all, I figured you'd appreciate the Christmas story. Getting it out into the world, the real reason for the season and all. And like I said, I love your voice!"

He seemed to be really considering it now, staring back outside for a beat before rolling his eyes and nodding.

I smiled. Golden. I stuck out my hand. "I owe you!"

Johnny took it, and held it, then pulled me in and grinned. "Yes, you will."

I told him the details for the rehearsal and said goodbye.

Then I sat at the diner bar and ordered that burger and fries that I'd been hankering for.

Because boy, did I need that lunch after the morning!

Slept horrible that night. Too jumpy about getting to the practice that morning. Thankfully, we got all the parts lined up, with a big shout-out to Katrina who found my angelic choir, working her Mill Creek magic on Max Blade, Old Man

Freddy Nugent, and Mayor Goodall of all people. Not enough for a choir, but three was better than none. Never did get the Three Wise Men, which was fine. I did get our baby Jesus, though. The Robertson's newborn. Ken and Barbara were ecstatic about it too, but we used a baby doll from the nursery as a stand in. No sense putting a baby through the day!

Fixed me up a plate of eggs and toast and washed it down with a half pot of coffee. Put on another while I showered and dressed, then brought it along in a thermal mug for the road ahead that stretched just outside my parsonage door.

Thankfully, the Lord sought fit to keep the lake effect snow bands from dumping even more than the record he'd already let loose on us the past few weeks. Not that I minded. Always thought the days between Thanksgiving and Christmas should be as snow-filled as possible, maybe even to New Year. Then, after the holidays, let the jet stream bend toward Canada the rest of the year and deal with the cold and snow. They were made for that sort of thing.

A little before 9 a.m., I got the lights turned on in the sanctuary and heat cranked for the day that was proving to be a bitter one. Polar vortex, they called it. Which was fitting. Why not add that to the virus and murder hornets and contested election that had messed with our heads all year?

Five till, the cast started rolling in, slowly but surely as I finished making coffee. By five after, the first few pew rows in the sanctuary were filled with the Junction's finest. My stomach was a bundle of nerves now, and jacked up on too much coffee, but I stepped up to the plate before we got to it to rally the troops.

"First of all, I just wanted to say thanks for your help. I know some of you were arm-wrestled into this—"

"Strong-armed, more like it," Gideon complained; Annabelle hit his arm and frowned.

"I prefer to frame it as sweet-talked, myself," I said, throwing Gideon a wink. "But seriously, thank you. I know how special the yearly Junction Christmas pageant is to the town and its history, stretching back to its founding, isn't that right?"

"Clear back to that first Christmas in 1876," Mayor Goodall said.

I whistled. "Which means we've got quite the legacy to fulfill! And I know the Junction typically puts on a non-sectarian program, more Santa and elves than Jesus and shepherds. But hey, you snagged a pastor into this thing, Mayor. So sue me."

The group chuckled. Mayor Goodall shook a finger at me and laughed, nodding in agreement.

I smiled and continued, "We're not making a big deal of it all, and there won't be any come-to-Jesus moment afterward. Just telling the story of Jesus' birth and then a time of town fellowship afterward with Christmas cookies and candy."

"No sermon by preacherman?" Max said. "Aww, nuts. How disappointing."

"Well, I've pretty much given up any hope of converting you, Max, so don't worry."

"Amen to that!" Old Man Nugent said.

Now Max hit his arm and frowned. The man shielded himself and chuckled.

"Alright, I know it's early," I went on, "and you've probably got stuff to do this last weekend before Christmas, so enough talk from me. How about we get to it?" The group nodded and stretched and brought out their spiral-bound scripts. "How about we take it from the top, Johnny?"

Johnny Pope nodded and stood, then sauntered up to a stool on the platform at the front. Curling back the first few pages, he cleared his throat and began reading the Christmas story from the Gospel of Luke: "'*In those days Caesar Augustus issued a decree that a census should be taken of the entire Roman world. This was the first census that took place while Quirinius was governor of Syria. And everyone went to their own town to register.*'"

He stopped, the cue for the other actors.

Who weren't stepping up to the plate.

"Max, Freddy, Mayor Goodall," I said, "that's your cue."

The trio shuffled to the front, clearly not paying attention. This was going to be a long morning.

"We don't have any lines," the mayor said, who I tapped to double as the census taker. Seemed right. The other two angels were pulling double-duty as Roman citizens.

"You still gotta act it out, knuckleheads," Johnny complained with irritation.

"Hey, who are you calling knucklehead, knucklehead?" Max shot back.

"Alright, alright," I said, putting up a hand. Then I addressed the group, "Not many have lines, but we're still going through the motions, so we know what to expect next week. Alright?"

The group offered a grumbly agreement.

I pointed to the three angels doubling as Roman census taker and citizens, then motioned for them to get on with it. They did, the mayor at a table and the pair registering as citizens. Then they stiffly shuffled to the side.

Johnny sipped from a bottle of water, then continued,

"'*So Joseph also went up from the town of Nazareth in Galilee to Judea, to Bethlehem the town of David, because he belonged to the house and line of David. He went there to register with Mary, who was pledged to be married to him and was expecting a child.*'"

Out came Gideon and Annabelle from stage left, her arm in his and the pair smiling at one another while Annabelle rubbed her belly. They were surprisingly comfortable with one another. If I hadn't known better, I would have assumed they were dating. Maybe they were.

"Now, Annabelle, in the production," I announced, "you'll be riding on a donkey and you'll be pulling her along somewhat, Gideon."

"A donkey?" Annabelle exclaimed.

"You never said anything about a donkey," Gideon said.

I furrowed my brow, feigning confusion. "I didn't? Huh. Well, there you have it." Of course, I hadn't said anything for fear they wouldn't have agreed to play the part!

Annabelle looked at Gideon. "I don't know about this now. Not a big fan of farm animals."

"Oh, it's domesticated, so no worries," I said, waving my hand as if it wasn't a big deal, then motioning to Johnny. "Continue."

Johnny glanced at the star-attraction pair, then gave his head a shake. "'*While they were there, the time came for the baby to be born, and she gave birth to her firstborn, a son. She wrapped him in cloths and placed him in a manger, because there was no room for them at the inn.*'"

"'*Guest room available for them,*'" I corrected. "You were probably reciting from memory."

Johnny furrowed his brow and squinted at the script. "Well, I'll be...What happened to the inn?"

"It really wasn't an inn. Not like we think of it, anyway."

"So no Motel 6 on Bethlehem's Route 66," Max quipped.

"Something like that."

Johnny scoffed. "Just like you Protestants to change the Scriptures..."

"I heard that," I said with a smile. "Let's take it from the top."

Johnny cleared his throat and nodded. "*While they were there, the time came for the baby to be born, and she gave birth to her firstborn, a son. She wrapped him in cloths and placed him in a manger, because there was no—*" he looked at me, then finished, "*'guest room available for them.'*"

I gave a thumbs up.

"*'And there were shepherds living out in the fields near-by,'*" he went on, "*'keeping watch over their flocks at night.'*"

Gerald Roller, Mill Creek Junction police chief, had been snagged as a chief shepherd, and he was leading some of the teenagers in the church. They came ambling out as Max Blade joined them.

I put up a hand. "Too soon, Max. Give 'em ten."

"Minutes?"

"Seconds."

He nodded, and Chief Roller and the boys ambled out holding staffs.

Johnny said, "*An angel of the Lord appeared to them, and the glory of the Lord shone around them, and they were terrified. But the angel said to them.*"

I motioned for Max to step out now.

He did, exclaiming with a raised hand, "*'Do not be*"

afraid. I bring you good news that will cause great joy for all the people.'"

He stopped and looked at me. Not bad, actually. I motioned for him to continue.

Max swallowed and nodded. *"'Today in the town of David a Savior has been born to you; he is the Messiah, the Lord. This will be a sign to you: You will find a baby wrapped in cloths and lying in a manger.'"*

After which Johnny narrated, *"'Suddenly a great company of the heavenly host appeared with the angel, praising God and saying:'"*

Now the angelic choir, which was more a trio, now that I thought of it, stepped forward and announced, *"'Glory to God in the highest heaven—'"*

I interrupted, "A little more gusto, this time, alright?"

"Gusto?" Mayor Goodall said, voice laced with annoyance.

"Yeah, with passion, feeling! You're an angel of the Lord, with the best announcement ever! So maybe put your diaphragm into it."

The three glanced at one another and shrugged, then said again:

"'Glory to God in the highest heaven, and on earth peace to those on whom his favor rests.'"

Much more gusto. I gave a thumbs up and motioned for Johnny.

"'When the angels had left them and gone into heaven, the shepherds said to one another...'"

There was silence, then a shuffling as Chief Roller stepped up to the plate now.

I rolled my eyes and put a hand to my head, wishing people would pay attention and follow along in their scripts!

"'*Let's go to Bethlehem,*'" Chief Roller said, very monotonously, I might add, with stiff back and arms at his side, "'*and see this thing that has happened, which the Lord has told us about.*'"

Johnny continued, "'*So they hurried off—*'"

"Hold up Mary and Joseph." I forced a smile and brought that hand to my head again, frustration building at the band of merry men who'd been assembled to share the greatest story ever told, announcing the greatest news ever.

But then I took a breath and decided on a different tack.

I said, "Alright, let's have a coffee break." For my sake as much as theirs! "Then we'll run through it one more time."

A chorus of mumbly grumbles rippled through the group.

"This ain't Broadway, preacherman!" Max complained. "Can't we call it good?"

I crossed my arms. "Now what would your Blade ancestors say to that?" He went to answer, but I wouldn't let him. "I seem to recall you trying to live up to their reputation one short Halloween ago, and how some certain individuals pulled together to end the traditional Junction trick-or-treat bash with a bang."

Gideon leaned over to Max. "He's got you there."

Max threw him a frown.

"I know you've got things to do this afternoon, and I won't keep you long. So can we take five and then get back to it for one more run?"

"How about ten?" Max countered.

I smiled and nodded. "Take fifteen and we'll run through it just once. Promise."

Everyone agreed and headed into the fellowship hall for the coffee I'd brewed earlier and some cookies and pastries Katrina had set out.

Then we came back together and ran through it all once more from the top, hitting some bumps along the way but better than the first time. Everyone was ready for their part, on cue, and without complaint. Hit all the right lines and moves. Which gave me hope we might pull off this Christmas pageant yet.

By the grace of God...

Today was the day. And if I was nervous the day of practice, that had nothing on what I was feeling that morning. Could hardly touch the egg sandwich I'd made, and coffee didn't sit well either. I'd have to go into the day without my power breakfast and riding on nothing but a Clif Bar. But off I went down my snow-covered parish house walkway, nearly biffing it on a patch of unseen ice.

Hoped it wasn't a sign of things to come.

I arrived as Mill Creek Baptist folks were putting the finishing touches on the inside decorations. Place smelled like a cookie factory smack dab in the middle of a North Pole forest. It was amazing!

Three fresh-cut Christmas trees at the entrance decked out in red, green, and white ornaments and cranberry-red beaded garland on top of miles of garland running the length of the ceiling. Seven tables held piles of Christmas cookies dripping with icing, all in the shape of candy canes, Christmas trees, stars, Santa and his reindeer—this was on top of bar cookies with M&Ms, drop cookies decked out in powder sugar, ginger snaps, snickerdoodle, and plates of brownies. Felt myself growing a Santa belly just taking in the sugary smell!

But I was nervous as a priest in a brothel. Or perhaps a reverend before his first ever town Christmas pageant!

Coming up behind me, Katrina rested a hand on my shoulder and handed me a cup of coffee. "Figured you'd need this. And this." She handed me a Santa Christmas cookie, but instead of wearing his trademark red suit and red hat, he had on a black one with a fedora.

I chuckled. "Looks like Santa had a run-in with a French tailor."

She laughed. "It's supposed to be you, Pastor Young. Made special for today."

Wow, how touching! I gave her a gentle hug, carefully holding my coffee and cookie. "Thanks, Katrina. For all of this! My goodness, does it look amazing. And that's not even touching on what you did to assemble the cast for this afternoon."

"Well, the main event was all you, Peter. Speaking of which, you should probably gather the farm animals. About ready to get the show on the road."

I bit my head off before anyone else did and washed the cookie down with a swig of coffee. "Probably right. Wish me luck!"

"Naw, you don't need it. You'll be fine."

Shoving the rest of my cookie in my mouth and downing it with lukewarm, mostly bad church coffee, I hustled off to the meeting room behind the sanctuary stage, praying she was right.

Entering the backroom, I was pleased to see everyone already gathered. Or most everyone. Suppose we had thirty minutes or so until showtime, but it was good to see most everyone already in costume or getting there.

Annabelle was looking every bit like Mary. She was with

Barbara, who was holding her son, the Baby Jesus stand-in. Then Chief Roller and Mayor Chet Goodall yakking it up, along with Old Man Nugent and Johnny Pope. The teenagers who'd been roped in as shepherds, and then—

"Wait…" This wasn't right.

I counted everyone again, checking off the names in my head.

Missing two.

Nearly dropped my bad church coffee. I exclaimed, "Where's Gideon and Max?"

The group stopped what they were doing and glanced around, seemingly not noticing their absence.

Annabelle explained, "I think they were coming together. Max was picking up Gideon at his house."

"Well, they ain't here!" I rushed back out into the sanctuary, stopping short at the door. Place was filling up now. Big time. Nearly every seat being picked off by Junction folks coming out for the Mill Creek Christmas pageant.

And me without Joseph and the Angel of the Lord!

"I'm gonna ring that Max Blade's ne—"

Catching sight of Max running down the aisle in a bedsheet cut me off. Gideon was close behind in his blue-robe costume.

I took a deep breath and downed the rest of my coffee, ushering in the two stragglers. Thank you, Lord!

"Sorry about that, preacherman," Max said, out of breath and all flustered.

"No problem. What happened?"

"Golden Nugget's not so golden," Gideon sneered, meeting up with Annabelle and Barbara.

"Don't dog on the Nugget, dude!" Max said. He turned to me. "Car trouble. But we got it worked out."

"Not a problem," I said, trying to catch my own breath.

"Just take a deep breath. You're here now. That's what matters."

He offered a weak smile and nodded, wandering over to the other two angels.

Glancing at my watch, I took one more peek outside.

Nearly full now, and nearly time.

Closing my eyes and taking another calming breath, I turned to the crew. "Can I have everyone's attention?" They silenced themselves and turned my way. "Thanks again for helping me out this year. I know I strong-armed you a bit getting you to sign up—"

"Yeah, killer right hook, kid," Johnny Pope said, getting laughs from the others.

"But he didn't have nothing on his assistant, Katrina," said Mayor Goodall. "Now there's a strong arm!"

The others laughed along. It was good to hear everyone in good spirits. Hoped that translated into a good show.

"As I was saying..." I continued, "Just wanted to say thanks for the help, and for giving Mill Creek a chance to remember what this season is about after the year we've had. The real reason for the season, as they say."

"Oh, yeah, preacherman," Max said, "and what's that?"

I paused, considering his question. I went with, "Hope. And I don't know about you, but after this year, with the virus and protests and election—"

"Don't forget the murder hornets!" Annabelle said.

"And turning forty during lockdown!" Gideon added.

We all laughed. Boy, had it been a year.

"And all that!" I said. "Given all that, I'd say we need a bit of that as we end the year." The room agreed. "So let's give it to the Junction, alright?"

Everyone cheered, and we got into our positions for the

show that would only come together because of the Lord's good graces.

I got into position off-stage just as the house lights dimmed. Only light left now was the sun from the stained glass fighting for a hearing and a single spotlight on a stool set off to the side for our narrator.

I took a breath and rubbed my hands together. Showtime...

Johnny was looking mighty sharp in his black suit as he walked up to his stool. Didn't take him for a shirt and tie kind of guy, but he pulled it off well. He carried a black binder with him and set it on a music stand. He paused for a breath, looking out into the room, then he began.

"*In those days Caesar Augustus issued a decree that a census should be taken of the entire Roman world. This was the first census that took place while Quirinius was governor of Syria. And everyone went to their own town to register. He went there to register with Mary, who was pledged to be married to him and was expecting a child.*'"

Cue another spotlight at the opposite end of the stage. Mayor Goodall was seated at a table wearing a robe, pointing to a pad of paper with one hand and a pen with the other. Max Blade and Old Man Freddy Nugent were also in place, arms crossed and grumbling to one another. Max snatched the pen from Goodall and started scribbling, then handed it to Freddy, who did likewise.

It got a little laugh. More importantly, scene one was complete.

My stomach could start loosening a bit. We were right on track.

The light faded at the one end, and Johnny continued from the other: "*So Joseph also went up from the town of*

Nazareth in Galilee to Judea, to Bethlehem the town of David, because he belonged to the house and line of David.'"

Now a light shone down at the back of the sanctuary. Clearly unexpected, because the audience mumbled and spun around for a look.

To find Gideon O'Donnell leading a donkey with Annabelle Kirkland seated sideways on top, holding her very pregnant-looking belly. He had on a blue robe with tan slacks, and she was wearing a white dress edged by crimson —a nice picture of her purity, her virginity, while nodding toward the bloody, sacrificial death of her son.

The audience loved it, *oohing* and *ahhing* and laughing good-naturedly and pointing at the pair as they walked down the aisle.

Right until the donkey let rip an echoey sound reserved for the barnyard, and clumps of the animal's breakfast came out the other end in the middle of the center aisle.

"Aww, crap..." I muttered, mortified but suddenly realizing the irony. Couldn't help but giggle now and had to keep myself from cracking up.

Crap is right! That'll leave a stain, but the pair kept at it.

Whether from being the pros they are or because they were oblivious, it wasn't clear. But they kept toward the front, the spotlight following them.

The sanctuary filled with laughter as it filled with the distinct smell of that crap. Shortly, Mary and Joseph and the offending donkey reached the front.

A light at the center faded up to a small traditional-looking nativity set, wood beams stained darkly angled at the top and straw piled on top for a roof. Same dark-stained wood was at the back, bales of hay piled in front and around a cattle trough for the manger.

Someone dressed as a shepherd was at the front to take

the donkey and help Annabelle to the ground. She dismounted perfectly, gracefully. Which allowed me to stop holding my breath.

She and Gideon went to the manger while the stagehand took the donkey off to the side.

Johnny continued, "'*While they were there, the time came for the baby to be born, and she gave birth to her first-born, a son.*'"

As if the Spirit of the Lord himself intervened, a baby offered a cry from the front center—from the manger. Ken and Barbara's newborn had been placed inside and he was now making noise.

Annabelle picked him up, the audience craning toward the front and *ahhing* with approval at the reveal, whispering to one another and pointing to the front.

I smiled. That was my idea. And it worked! I threw up a quick prayer that the little one would pull it together, and he did. Annabelle managed to quiet him as Johnny continued narrating.

He said, "'*She wrapped him in cloths and placed him in a manger, because there was no guest room available for them.*'"

Guest room was said with emphasis, as if for my benefit. I grinned from the side. Apparently you could teach an old dog new tricks.

The center light faded down and a new light faded up on stage right, opposite from Johnny. Where the shepherds, led by Chief Roller, were congregating with three sheep in front of bales of hay stacked by twos.

With real sheep!

More approving *ahhs* and *oohs* and laughter rose from the audience, a poor sheep *baaing* with disapproval at the sudden attention.

I prayed for no more crap from this crowd of barnyard animals, or else cleanup was going to be more than I bargained for!

"'*And there were shepherds living out in the fields nearby,*'" Johnny went on narrating, "'*keeping watch over their flocks at night. An angel of the Lord appeared to them—*'"

Cue the first of the Three Stooges rising from behind bales of hay. Which got quite the approving laugh and bouts of cheer from the Junction folk. Another idea I had to make it all work.

"'*—and the glory of the Lord shone around them,*'" Johnny continued, "*and they were terrified. But the angel said to them...*'"

There was silence. Too much silence. Awkward silence. Until Chief Roller muttered something under his breath and I heard a quiet, "Oh, crap. That'd be me!"

But Max came through, announcing with gusto: "Do not be afraid, Chief. Err, Mister Shepherd man."

I chuckled to myself and shook my head. Oh, Max. God love ya! A few others seemed to feel the same, groans and laughter thrown up from the audience.

He cleared his throat and continued with a raised arm, "'*I bring you good news that will cause great joy for all the people. Today in the town of David a Savior has been born to you; he is the Messiah, the Lord. This will be a sign to you: You will find a baby wrapped in cloths and lying in a manger.*'"

Now Mayor Goodall and Old Man Nugent stood from behind the bales of hay next to Max.

Johnny said, "'*Suddenly a great company of the heavenly host appeared with the angel, praising God and saying...*'"

"'*Glory to God in the highest heaven,*'" the men announced with a certain amount of glee and authority behind it, "*and on earth peace to those on whom his favor rests.*'"

Several claps arose from the audience, followed by more until the house was brought down. Max took a bow before Goodall and Freddy clenched both shoulders and pushed him down behind the bales of hay—to more laughter and claps.

"'*When the angels had left them and gone into heaven, the shepherds said to one another...*'" Johnny said from stage left.

Chief Roller cleared his throat and exclaimed, "'*Let's go to Bethlehem and see this thing that has happened, which the Lord has told us about.*'"

Not bad. More excitement than I was used to from the police chief, which was fine. I'll take it!

Nearly to the finish line now. My palms were wet and shirt sticking to my back, but what mattered was it was coming together. It *had* come together! All thanks to these dear, normal, ordinary souls. Which pretty much fit the bill for who showed up to that first Christmas—except perhaps the angels.

"Thank you, Lord..." I muttered as we hit the home stretch.

Johnny continued narrating, "'*So they hurried off and found Mary and Joseph, and the baby, who was lying in the manger.*'"

The center light faded back up, and the shepherds shuffled across the stage to the nativity barn. Chief Roller went to one knee in front of Mary, who was cradling Baby Jesus, with Joseph standing behind her. The other shepherds followed suit, the four of them bowing their heads. Didn't think that was in the script, but I liked it. Whether spontaneous or planned, it was a moving image, the shepherds bowing before the infant who was the King of kings and Lord of lords.

"'*When they had seen him, they spread the word concerning what had been told them about this child, and all who heard it were amazed at what the shepherds said to them.*'"

Now the shepherds left Gideon and Annabelle, and the pair stood together beneath the light. Mary holding the baby close to her chest, who was fairing surprisingly well. And Joseph kneeling now close to both, his one arm wrapped around her back and the other resting on the baby's head.

"'*But Mary treasured up all these things and pondered them in her heart,*'" Johnny said, drawing the pageant to a close.

His light faded down, but the light at the center kept at it, and for a good three minutes and sixteen seconds. Sort of a random seeming time, but I did that on purpose. It symbolized one of the greatest verses in the Bible, John 3:16.

> *For God so loved the world that he gave his*
> *one and only Son, that whoever believes*
> *in him shall not perish but have eternal*
> *life.*

No one knew but me, and that was fine. I did want the time to stand, however, to let people ponder what they had seen. Like the shepherds, like Mary herself.

But then the lights faded to darkness, and the verse was displayed behind the pair on the dark wood back. Probably stepped over the line a bit, proselytizing a bit too much given the nature of the town pageant. Oh, well! It was there only ten seconds, and it served as a reminder of why we celebrated the season to begin with.

Not sure how many people noticed, because the sanctuary erupted with cheers and applause, sustained for several minutes. The house lights came up, and the cast came out to be recognized, which seemed to ratchet it up even more, the Junction rising to their feet to offer their appreciation for the performance.

My throat constricted now with a sudden rise of emotion as the crew took their bows and received the applause, and rightly so. They'd done it! Boy, was I proud of them. And mighty grateful. These ordinary, normal folk of Mill Creek Junction help me tell the original Christmas story, whether believer or not.

Aside from the angels, the God-with-us-God showed up in the most ordinary and normal of ways: being birthed as a baby boy, and in a cattle trough! Not only that, but he was born to peasant teenagers in occupied Judea. Not to royalty but to a carpenter and a disgraced young girl who had become pregnant before marriage—miraculously so, through the power of the Holy Spirit, but she was shunned for it.

Who would have thought this was how God was going to rescue the world? Nope, no one. Yet there it was, acted out before Mill Creek Junction in the sanctuary of a humble Baptist church in small-town America.

A reminder that he still shows up to the ordinary and normal, and in the most ordinary and normal of ways.

Which was the entire point of running around the last few weeks, the stress and work. The real reason for the season, as they say.

Wasn't just about filling time and completing my civic duty. Nope, not in the slightest!

It was about putting on full display the magical, revolutionary story showcasing the wonders of God's love—and the lengths he went to show it.

There it was, that story, that love. At a Mill Creek Junction Christmas pageant of all places—with me as director!

Go figure.

Explore More of Mill Creek Junction

Welcome to a new story world inspired by such fictional towns as John Grisham's Clanton, Mississippi, and Stephen King's Castle Rock, Maine.

Get to know this world one character, one setting, one event and situation at a time. You're sure to find some of your own story in theirs, while being entertained and inspired for the journey.

Visit www.millcreekjunction.com for more details about the world and a list of short and long-form fiction, following the lives of real people living life and exploring faith.

Get Your Free Thriller

Building a relationship with my readers is one of my all-time favorite joys of writing! Once in a while I like to send out a newsletter with giveaways, free stories, pre-release content, updates on new books, and other bits on my stories.

Join my insider's group for updates, giveaways, and your free novel—a full-length action-adventure story in my *Order of Thaddeus* thriller series. Just tell me where to send it.

Follow this link to subscribe:
www.jabouma.com/free

About the Author

J. A. Bouma believes nobody should have to read bad religious fiction—whether it's cheesy plots with pat answers or misrepresentations of the Christian faith and the Bible. So he wants to do something about it by telling compelling, propulsive stories that thrill as much as inspire, while offering a dose of insight along the way.

As a former congressional staffer and pastor, and award-nominated bestselling author of over forty religious fiction and nonfiction books, he blends a love for ideas and adventure, exploration and discovery, thrill and thought. With graduate degrees in Christian thought and the Bible, and armed with a voracious appetite for most mainstream genres, he tells stories you'll read with abandon and recommend with pride—exploring the tension of faith and doubt, spirituality and culture, belief and practice, and the gritty drama that is our collective pilgrim story.

When not putting fingers to keyboard, he loves vintage jazz vinyl, a glass of Malbec, and an epic read—preferably together. He lives in Grand Rapids with his wife, two kiddos, and rambunctious boxer-pug-terrier.

www.jabouma.com • jeremy@jabouma.com

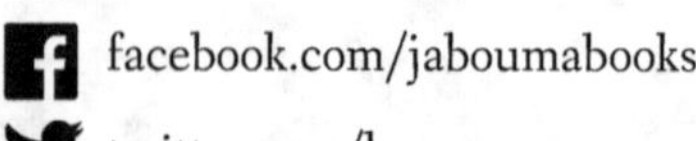

facebook.com/jaboumabooks
twitter.com/bouma
amazon.com/author/jabouma

Also by J. A. Bouma

Nobody should have to read bad religious fiction—whether it's cheesy plots with pat answers or misrepresentations of the Christian faith and the Bible. So J. A. Bouma tells compelling, propulsive stories that thrill as much as inspire, offering a dose of insight along the way.

Order of Thaddeus **Action-Adventure Thriller Series**

Holy Shroud • Book 1

The Thirteenth Apostle • Book 2

Hidden Covenant • Book 3

American God • Book 4

Grail of Power • Book 5

Templars Rising • Book 6

Rite of Darkness • Book 7

Gospel Zero • Book 8

The Emperor's Code • Book 9

Deadly Hope • Book 10

Fallen Ones • Book 11

Silas Grey Collection 1 (Books 1-3)

Silas Grey Collection 2 (Books 4-6)

Silas Grey Collection 3 (Books 7-9)

Backstories: Short Story Collection 1

Martyrs Bones: Short Story Collection 2

Ichthus Chronicles **Sci-Fi Apocalyptic Series**

Apostasy Rising / Season 1, Episode 1

Apostasy Rising / Season 1, Episode 2

Apostasy Rising / Season 1, Episode 3

Apostasy Rising / Season 1, Episode 4

Apostasy Rising / Full Season 1 (Episodes 1 to 4)

Apocalypse Rising / Season 2, Episode 1

Apocalypse Rising / Season 2, Episode 2

Apocalypse Rising / Season 2, Episode 3

Apocalypse Rising / Season 2, Episode 4

Apocalypse Rising / Full Season 2 (Episodes 1 to 4)

Faith Reimagined **Spiritual Coming-of-Age Series**

A Reimagined Faith • Book 1

A Rediscovered Faith • Book 2

Mill Creek Junction **Short Story Series**

Get all the latest short stories at: www.millcreekjunction.com

Find all of my latest book releases at: www.jabouma.com

www.ingramcontent.com/pod-product-compliance
Lightning Source LLC
Chambersburg PA
CBHW071811190726
48292CB00008B/2798